"Do You Believe I'm Trustworthy?"

Hank's amber eyes bored into Laura's.

She gave him a probing look. "Aren't you?"

"Yes, as a matter of fact, I am." His voice was low, attractive, sexy. "Does being trustworthy mean I can't carry out my plans for the two of us?"

"Plans?"

Hank's smile was slow, exciting, unnerving. He cocked an eyebrow and raised his arm in a smooth, deceptively lazy motion. His warm fingers brushed the curve of her throat.

"What are you doing?"

"Didn't you just say you trusted me?"

"Yes, but . . ." Her voice dwindled to a rough whisper as his hand slid around her nape. "Hank?"

His voice dropped to a caressing murmur. "I'm going to kiss you."

"Wh-what if I don't want you to?"

"In that case," he murmured, his lips within a breath of hers, "I'm afraid I will have to insist."

Dear Reader:

Happy Valentine's Day!

It takes two to tango, and we've declared 1989 as the "Year of the Man" at Silhouette Desire. We're honoring that perfect partner, the magnificent male, the one without whom there would *be* no romance. January marks the beginning of a twelve-month extravaganza spotlighting one book each month as a tribute to the Silhouette Desire hero—our *Man of the Month*!

Created by your favorite authors, these men are utterly irresistible. Joan Hohl's Mr. February is every woman's idea of the perfect Valentine, and March, traditionally the month that "comes in like a lion, goes out like a lamb," brings a hero to match with Jennifer Greene's Mr. March.

Don't let these men get away!

Yours,

Isabel Swift
Senior Editor & Editorial Coordinator

JOAN HOHL
The Gentleman Insists

Silhouette Desire

Published by Silhouette Books New York

America's Publisher of Contemporary Romance

SILHOUETTE BOOKS
300 East 42nd St., New York, N.Y. 10017

ISBN: 0-373-05475-0

First Silhouette Books printing February 1989

JOAN HOHL,

a Gemini and an inveterate daydreamer, says she always has her head in the clouds. An avid reader all her life, she discovered romances about ten years ago. "And as soon as I read one," she confesses, "I was hooked." Now an extremely prolific author, she is thrilled to be getting paid for doing exactly what she loves best.

For my new gentleman,
my grandson Cammeron.
Welcome, love.

One

She was a knockout from any angle. Feeling as if his hormones were rushing together and his senses falling apart, Hank Branson studied the woman from every angle known to man. Since his arrival had not yet been noticed, he stood in the shadows of the small foyer of the elegant town house, taking advantage of the opportunity for a more encompassing inspection.

She was worth the effort. Hank correctly judged her to be about five feet six or so inches tall. Her body was slender but nicely rounded, without a hint of the flat angular look of the constant dieter. Her skin was fair, translucent, and an interesting contrast to her flowing mane of gleaming dark brown hair. She was attired in casual splendor in the colors of the season; slim raw silk slacks in daffodil yellow complemented a smooth silk green-on-green tailored shirt. A wide lilac-tinted soft leather belt dramatically defined her small waist, while matching strappy sandals revealed her slim feet. And when she moved... Hank swallowed a groan. Her body moved with a fluid grace that conjured erotic images of warm dark nights and even warmer satin sheets.

Suddenly uncomfortable, Hank set the expensive bottle of wine he'd brought as a hostess gift on the floor and shrugged out of the suede jacket he'd worn against the nip in the late afternoon spring air. His movement caught the attention of another woman in the animated group gathered in the long room. A smile of recognition tilted the corners of his mouth and sparked a glow in his amber-colored eyes as he watched this younger woman detach herself from her companions and walk to the woman he'd been observing. It was then that Hank noticed the resemblance between the two.

Sisters? he wondered, scrutinizing the pair. With their heads together in murmured conversation, the likeness was obvious: height, figure, skin tone, hair color. But there were differences, as well. Though more than merely pretty, the younger woman had the lanky energetic look that betrayed her nineteen years, whereas the other possessed not only a breath-stopping beauty but a sophisticated self-confident maturity. Hank had known the younger woman, Megan Seaton, for some months, ever since he'd hired her as a part-time secretary the previous fall. She had mentioned having one sibling, a sister two years her senior, who was married and the mother of a seven-month-old daughter. Could the woman he had been admiring possibly be Megan's sister?

Hank's stomach lurched with the thought. The glow in his eyes dimmed as he saw the woman glance in his direction, a bright impersonal smile curving her gorgeous mouth. Although she appeared older, with more composure than most twenty-one-year-old women, she had to be Megan's sister, he concluded, feeling his spirits plunge. But, if the beauty was Megan's sister, where was his hostess, Megan's mother?

As the two women moved toward him, Hank skimmed a narrow-eyed glance over the faces of the guests. His gaze came to an abrupt halt on the profile of an older woman holding court from the straight-backed chair she was seated in near the front of the room. Here, again, the resemblance was unavoidable. He guessed this woman to be somewhere in her fifties, but it was hard to be certain because she had the ageless beauty of patrician features and smooth young-looking skin.

Hank hadn't been overly enthusiastic about attending the gathering in the first place. Yet, having neither plans for the holiday nor the heart to refuse Megan's sweetly proffered invitation, he had agreed to join her and her family in their suburban Philadelphia home for what he believed would be a traditional holiday meal.

He had envisioned the family gathered around a dining room table adorned with spring flowers and the obligatory basket of colored eggs, sharing a baked ham or possibly spring lamb with mint jelly. He had certainly not expected the underplayed elegance of the town house he had walked into—at the invitation of the matronly housekeeper who had opened the door for him. Nor had he expected the crush of well-dressed guests or the long obviously catered buffet table positioned at the end of the room, behind which two white-jacketed waiters served generous portions of gourmet food. And, most of all, Hank had never expected to set eyes on a woman and experience a sensation that could be compared to being mule kicked in the solar plexus.

Hank didn't like the sensation, but there it was, a strange hollow feeling in his gut, yawning ever wider as the woman drew closer to him. His eyes glittering like the stone they resembled, Hank settled his gaze on the two women coming to a stop in front of him. An odd bolt of pleasure-pain seared through his chest as his glance collided with the woman's bright hazel eyes before ricocheting to Megan's animated face. In that instant he had a vague premonition of what Megan was going to say for, in the brief but close-up look he'd had of her, Hank knew the other woman was nearer to his own thirty-six years than to Megan's sister's age.

"Happy Easter, Hank," Megan greeted him with a warm smile. "I'm glad you decided to come." Her smile tilted impishly as she glanced sideways at the other woman. "We're glad you decided to come," she corrected, indicating her companion. "I'd like you to meet my mother, Laura Seaton." She turned slightly. "Mother, this is my boss, Hank Branson."

"Mr. Branson. Welcome, and Happy Easter."

Hank saw the slim hand she extended—and grasped it. He heard her honey-voiced greeting—and responded properly to it. Afterward, he couldn't remember a word he'd said in those introductory moments. He was lost to the wild elation leaping through his entire being and the joyous litany singing in his head. *Megan's mother!* His premonition or intuition or whatever had been right on target. The beauty was not the married sister, mother of a seven-month-old daughter. She was Laura Seaton... Megan's mother! And he knew from information given by Megan that her mother was a widow.

Although Hank spent the afternoon and evening in hazy bemusement, bits and pieces of it stood out with clarity in his memory later, after he'd returned to the suddenly stark emptiness of his bachelor apartment.

He remembered asking her to call him Hank; she reciprocated by insisting he call her Laura. He recalled offering his gift of wine and Laura's gracious acceptance of it. He recollected the tingling awareness of his body to hers as he strolled by her side into the room. He heard again the honey-smooth sound of her voice as she introduced him to the other guests and recognized a faint echo of Laura's tone when he met Megan's sister, who, while lovely, paled in comparison to her mother. With amusement he remembered being introduced to the matriarch he had *thought* was Megan's mother, and learning she was actually *Laura's* mother.

Bits and pieces, all of them pleasant. While undressing for bed, Hank examined every bit and piece of memory, savoring each one with more appreciation than he had the delectable array of food he'd sampled from the buffet. The dinner table had included both baked ham and spring lamb with mint jelly, and was complemented by seasonal flowers and small baskets of artistically decorated eggs. But he saved the most pleasant of all the memories until after he slid naked between the cool sheets.

Laura. Hank rolled her name around in his mind, shivering with the image of her that rose before his closed eyelids. She was one stunning woman. And stunned barely defined his reaction to her.

And, although Hank couldn't recall one word he had spoken or heard from any other single person, he remembered each and every word he'd exchanged with Laura during those too brief moments she remained by his side.

"It was kind of you to invite me, a virtual stranger, into your home for what is traditionally a family holiday, Laura," he had said, wondering about the sharp sensation of warmth he experienced when the sleeve of his jacket brushed her arm.

"Megan said you would spend the day alone." She had tilted her head to look up at him. "No one should have to be alone on a holiday, Hank."

In that instant the warmth had spread throughout his body then centralized in his chest . . . and regions south. Hank suddenly had difficulty breathing. Was it the soft sound of compassion in her voice? Was it the light of caring in her beautiful eyes? Was it the soft curve of her mouth when she smiled? Hank didn't know. What he did know was that he had an odd feeling, an itchy feeling, deep down beneath the surface of his skin.

"I've been alone a long time, Laura," he'd replied, fighting an urge to scratch the itch by brushing his tingling mouth over hers. His intense stare must have relayed his desire, for her eyes flickered and she nearly wrung a groan from his tight throat by gliding her tongue nervously over her lips. Was Laura feeling a similar itch? *Had* she felt a similar itch? Hank asked himself again as he lay in the dark silent bedroom, re-living the exchange that had seemed polite and mundane but had concealed an immediate attraction he knew was mutual. Convinced that Laura had, and hoping she was still feeling a need to scratch, Hank frowned and moved restlessly beneath the light weight of the smooth sheet. He was puzzled by the intensity of his reaction to Laura Seaton. Being healthy and thoroughly male, he had naturally experienced moments of strong response to other women, but he had never felt anything like the immediate mind-divorcing sensation he'd felt at his first look at Laura.

His senses still reverberating from the effects of his response to her, Hank lay quiet, raking his mind for a reasonable explanation for his extraordinary reaction.

Without his conscious command, the image of Laura grew in his mind, an image so clear, so precise, it was an explanation of and by itself. His eyes shut tight, his breathing uneven, Hank took mental inventory of the cause of his physical dilemma.

With the clarity of memory, Laura stood before him, the contours of her body molded by clinging silk from her shoulders to her slender ankles. With his mind's eye, Hank sent a slow, hungry glance from her ankles up the long smooth line of her legs. Feeling his hunger grow, his inner eye outlined the gentle flare of her hips and her tucked-in waist, before moving on-ward and upward to her firm, perfectly propor-tioned, rounded breasts. Speculation about the feel and texture of her enticing breasts dried the moisture in his mouth and caused a tingling in his palms and fingers. In self-defense, he dragged his mental gaze from her chest to her face, examining her features in detail. Her nose was slender, her cheekbones high, her chin slightly squared and set at a determined angle. Her hazel eyes contained intelligence and the hidden shadows of sensuality, while her mouth... Lord! What he wouldn't do for a taste of her mouth!

Hank groaned aloud, and hearing the need strangling his voice, feeling the heat consuming his body, he banished the image by forcing his eyes to open. In a state of near shock, he realized that his heart was racing, his limbs were trembling and his skin was damp and clammy. His condition sharply reinforced his earlier contemplation; no, never before in his life had Hank experienced such intensity of response to any woman. He had wanted to possess her then, at once. He wanted to possess her here, and now.

As his heartbeat leveled and his body cooled, Hank promised himself the ultimate possession of Laura Seaton. With his goal firmly established in his being, he strained his faculties in an effort to remember any tidbit of information about her Megan had ever mentioned in passing.

As his memory unfurled, Hank recalled still more bits and pieces. Not long after he'd hired her, Megan had made an observation to the effect that his occupation of designer-contractor and her mother's of interior decorator were complementary to each other. After having the opportunity to see her work up close, in her own home, Hank was convinced of Laura's talent in her chosen field.

An interior designer. The thought struck a spark of inspiration that opened Hank's eyes and brought a contemplative smile to his thin masculine lips. On consideration, he concluded it would be advantageous to his business to have the sample home in his latest development professionally decorated. It would give him a plausible reason for contacting her. His smile deepening with satisfaction, Hank made a mental note to phone Laura to set up a professional conference meeting. Convinced the idea was vastly preferable to a more abrupt approach, he shut his eyes and continued to sift through his recollections.

Other than the fact that she had one sister, who was the elder by two years and married with one child, Hank's recall of the information Megan had given was cloudy at best. He was frowning in concentration when one remark the girl had made sprang clearly to his mind. Megan had told him that her father had died when she was three years old, leaving her mother a widow at the vulnerable age of twenty-three. If his figures were correct, and they inevitably were, that tallied to the mother being twenty years older than Megan, which meant that Laura was thirty-nine years old . . . and three years his senior. And, even after his minute inspection, discreetly accomplished, of course, he'd have sworn under oath that she was younger than him by at least the same number of years.

"Damn!" Jolting up in the bed, Hank laughed out loud.

In his unsolicited opinion, Laura Seaton was definitely not what any pollster might refer to as your average or typical grandmother!

"Laura Seaton scores yet another smashing success with her famous 'At home' holiday soirees!" Megan made the announcement in ringing tones as she dumped the contents of an ashtray into a large plastic trash bag.

As if on cue, her sister, Brooke, paused in the act of collecting glasses from the now littered buffet table and continued with the rave review. "As they reluctantly made their farewells, the happily stuffed guests were overheard singing the praises of the redoubtable hostess!"

From the front of the long room, where she was busy shifting furniture back into its proper position and plumping crushed toss pillows, Laura favored her giggling daughters with a dry look. "Redoubtable, indeed!" She laughed. "How very impressive you make me sound."

"Well, you are impressive," Megan called. "Everybody says you are."

Everybody? Laura mused, turning back to her work. *Did that include a certain somebody?* she wondered as she carefully dusted a gleaming table with a treated cloth.

Against her weary weakened will, an image of that certain somebody strolled nonchalantly into her mind. In an attempt to dislodge the too attractive vision, Laura shook her head sharply. Instead of vanishing, the vision smiled at her in the same breathtaking way the flesh-and-blood man had earlier that evening.

Go way! Laura silently ordered the vision.

The image of Hank Branson refused to dissolve.

Biting her lip to contain a groan, Laura tried to ignore the tantalizing vision by concentrating on rearranging a squat vase of violets on the freshly shined table.

A moment later a burst of giggles from the back of the room caught Laura's attention, and the image began to fade. Sighing in relief, she turned to look at her daughters. "Are you two drinking something back there?" she asked suspiciously.

Megan affected an injured expression. "Would we do a thing like that?"

"Yes." Laura's response was quick and unqualified.

Brooke's giggles bubbled over into delighted laughter. "We never could get away with anything with Mother," she said to her sister. "Show her the bottle, Megan."

Her grin teenage rakish, Megan grasped the slender neck of the dark glass bottle and held it aloft like a trophy. "There was a little less than a glass of wine left in the bottle that Hank brought you, I'm sorry to say, because this is really good stuff," she declared, smacking her lips comically. "I'd say my boss has excellent and expensive taste. On a scale of one to ten, I'd rate it a definite ten . . . maybe even eleven."

"On a scale of one to ten," Brooke observed, rolling her eyes appreciatively, "I'd rate your Mr. Branson a definite twenty, maybe twenty-five."

"At least," Megan agreed with an emphatic nod. "A lot of the time, whether he's in the office or on a job site, Hank is grouchy, impatient and demanding as hell." She flashed a grin at her sister. "But he is also sexy as the very devil . . . every minute of every day!"

With the mention of his name, the image of Hank Branson sprang back into Laura's mind, teasing her senses, depleting her strength. While the girls' animated voices faded into the background, an echo of Hank's deep slightly husky voice rang inside her head.

What had he said to her? Try as she might, Laura couldn't recall any but a few of his words, most particularly that of her own name. And the way he'd said her name! She shivered as she remembered the intonation of sensuality underlying Hank's deep tones.

"Mr. Branson didn't have much to say," Brooke observed. "Is he always that quiet?"

Laura's attention was again snared by hearing his name mentioned in a question reflecting her own thoughts, but this time his image remained firmly entrenched in her mind as she strained to hear Megan's response.

"Most of the time," Megan replied, laughing. "He really doesn't have to say much. All he has to do is give you what all his employees call 'the look' from those strange amber eyes of his." She exaggerated a shiver. "I mean, with one blazing look, that man can make you feel like either the lowest creature that ever presumed to crawl out of the slime or the greatest thing since safe sex!"

Laura's shiver intensified as she deliberately tuned out of the conversation. Recalling the effect of Hank's eyes on her own equilibrium, she accepted Megan's assertion without an instant of hesitation. In her mind, the eyes in the male image seemed to glitter with secret amusement.

As her attention strayed from what the young voices behind her were talking about, Laura continued working automatically. Telling herself she was merely curious about Hank Branson's apparent magnetism, she gave in to an unprecedented yet overriding urge to evaluate the persistent image of him.

Having stood and walked beside him, Laura knew he measured approximately six feet one or two inches in height. And, even from a distance, she had noticed that not an ounce of superfluous fat marred his muscular physique. The jacket to his stylish yet casual suit defined the breadth of his shoulders. Inside the open jacket, a fine cotton shirt clung lovingly to his broad chest. A narrow belt encircled his slender waist above trousers that molded his slim hips and outlined the length of his tautly muscled thighs and calves. His leather slip-on shoes had been buffed to a gleaming shine, which had made an immediate and favorable impression on her.

At first glance, his hair had not had a like impression on Laura. His hair was a toasty brown color, the ends tipped with gold but, though the shade was attractive, he wore it a trifle longer than the current fashion. The wind had tousled the silky strands, giving him a shaggy disreputable look. In retrospect, she reversed her opinion, deciding the shaggy look suited his overall appearance perfectly. The golden-tipped mane framed the commanding visage of a man unafraid of his individuality. His features were strong, his cheekbones prominent, his nose straight, his jaw hard and jutting beneath thin masculine lips. But most arresting of all were his riveting amber-colored eyes.

Hank Branson's eyes haunted her.

Suppressing a shiver, Laura consciously banished the image by tuning in to the conversation between her daughters.

"I was fascinated," Brooke was saying in a breathless tone. "I couldn't keep my eyes off of him, and while he didn't say much, he sure didn't miss anything!"

Sighing in defeat, Laura resigned herself to listening to her daughters discuss the man she had just decided not to think about.

Megan pretended shock. "Brooke Ann Seaton Tobias! You're a married woman! You're not supposed to be checking out other men anymore."

"Megan Marie Seaton, I'm married, not comatose," Brooke retorted. "And a normal woman would have to be flat-out unconscious not to notice a man as attractive and earthy-looking as Hank Branson."

"Yeah, Hank is rather delicious." Megan sighed dreamily. "I think I might be in love."

Though she was forced to concur with the first part of Megan's statement, Laura winced at her daughter's dramatic closing declaration.

"Again!" Brooke laughed. "What happened to that adorable premed student you were mad about last Christmas?"

You plucked the words right out of my mind, Laura thought with wry weariness.

"Oh, he's just a boy." Megan dismissed the young man with a toss of her long hair. "Hank's much more my type of man—mature, exciting, sexy."

"Oh, get real, Meg!" Brooke exclaimed on another burst of giggles.

Laura silently endorsed the advice.

"That mature, exciting, earthy-looking and sexy man is fathoms out of your league," Brooke said when she managed to control her laughter. "Why, he's old enough to be your father—*our* father!"

Is he? Laura frowned, feeling shocked at the intensity of her interest in Megan's answer.

"My dear, demented sister," Megan's tone was superior. "I happen to know that Hank is thirty-six."

Laura felt an odd sinking sensation on hearing that Hank was three years her junior.

"Correct me if I'm wrong," Meg went on, "but I do believe he was a mere fifteen when you were born, and too young to be your father."

Indeed! Laura agreed mutely.

"Which makes him seventeen years older than you," Brooke retaliated. "Which makes him old enough to be your father, and too old for you."

Bravo! Laura thought, applauding the logic of her older daughter's argument.

Caught short for a rebuttal, Megan went on packing trash into the plastic bag while casting fulminating looks at her sister's smug expression. Moments passed during which Laura felt that she could almost see the girl's mental gears grinding for an instant before her eyes telegraphed her cerebral success.

"Your argument is invalid," she said in a tone of dismissal, "simply because age is totally unimportant when it comes to love." She smiled triumphantly at Brooke, who was reduced to calling on the final arbiter for assistance.

"Mother!"

Laura had known it was coming, of course. From their very first real argument when they were still small children, her daughters had always called on her to resolve their differences. She never minded being placed in the position of referee. Quite the opposite, Laura had always felt pleased and honored by their trust in the fairness of her judgment. But tonight, unsettled by her own preoccupation with the man about whom the disagreement had erupted, Laura would have preferred to be excluded. Denying an urge to escape by admitting to the pain beginning to throb in her temples, she composed her features and smiled.

"You bellowed!" she asked serenely.

Brooke acknowledged the mild rebuke with a sheepish smile. "Sorry," she said with a sigh. "But, really, this daughter of yours is more of a trial than my infant."

"Umm." With the ambiguous murmur, Laura began walking toward the girls at the end of the room. The thought crossed her mind that it was not unlike crossing an invisible demarcation line between the neatly cleaned front of the room and the still cluttered section in the rear. It was always the same, she mused. Whenever her girls worked together they found something to squabble about, and though the work always got done, it usually required twice the amount of time to do than it would have taken Laura working by herself. As a rule, it didn't bother her. This evening was the exception to the rule, and all because of the subject of the girls' disagreement . . . one Hank Branson.

Due to her own extraordinary reaction to the man from the instant she'd glanced up to see him standing in the shadowed foyer, the last thing Laura wanted at that time of the night was to become embroiled in a discussion about him with her daughters, especially now, after hearing Megan's stark announcement. She would have to deal with her conflicting emotions, she knew that, but she preferred to do it from a distance of time, when she was alone and less tired and could think it through, make some sense of her jumbled feelings.

Realizing that they were unaware that their mother had overheard the most important part of their discussion, Laura smothered a sigh as she approached the buffet table and the two young women positioned on either side of it. "What is the bone of contention this time?" she asked.

"Megan's impossible!" Brooke exclaimed, as if her assertion explained the situation.

Her composure slipping, Laura drew a long impatient sigh. "Brooke, dear, I am very tired, and there is still a lot of cleaning up to do. Could you be just a little bit more specific?"

"Yes, of course," Brooke replied, but before she could go on, her sister rudely interrupted her.

"Don't you have to go upstairs to check on the baby?" Megan asked Brooke in an obvious attempt to change the topic of the conversation by distracting her sister.

"No." Brooke gave her sister a disdainful look. "If you'll remember, I checked on Heather a little while ago, and she was sleeping like—" she smiled "—a baby."

"Oh." Megan frowned with consternation, but then said quickly, "What about Don? I mean, isn't he—ah, waiting for you to come to bed?"

"No." Brooke's smile was chiding. "Don is as fast asleep as—" She broke off at the sound of her mother's harshly expelled breath.

"Now that we have established that both your husband and daughter are sleeping peacefully," Laura said grittily to Brooke, "Will you please get on with whatever it was you wanted to talk to me about?"

By their altered expressions, it was apparent that both girls recognized the edge in their mother's usually serene voice. She was about to reach the end of her patience, and they knew it. Megan subsided with a resigned sigh. Brooke hastened to explain.

"Mother, Megan thinks she's in love with Hank Branson, and the man is thirty-six years old!"

On having the information flung in her face, Laura felt a chill invade her body. It required every ounce of composure she possessed to look at her youngest child with an expression of calm inquiry. "Megan, is this true?"

"Except for one small detail, yes." Megan returned her mother's steady regard with mature directness. "You see," she went on, "I don't *think* I love Hank. I *know* I do."

Laura caught back a gasp caused by a sudden searing pain inside her chest. Unwilling to examine the reason for the inner violent reaction to her daughter's statement, she looked at Megan in despair.

"Honey, you're still very young," she began carefully.

"Mother!" Megan interrupted her. "I'm exactly the same age Brooke was when she married Don!"

"But Don is only four years older than Brooke," Laura pointed out gently. "And Mr. Branson is a mature, experienced—" That was as far as Megan allowed her to go.

"I know! I know!" the girl exclaimed. "I've already heard it all from Brooke!"

"Didn't I tell you?" Brooke interjected. "She's impossible. She won't listen!" Her voice was tight with genuine concern. "Mother, the man is thirty-six years old!"

"I realize the age difference, Brooke," Laura replied. "As I'm certain your sister does."

"Of course I do!" Megan's voice rose defensively. "I may only be nineteen, but I'm not a child. I know he's thirty-six. I know he's mature and experienced. I know! I know!"

Her composure shredding, Laura forced herself to ask the question burning in her mind. "Does Mr. Branson return your...feelings?" She waited in tense apprehension for an answer and felt an equal mixture of compassion and relief when her daughter's aggressive expression crumpled.

"I don't know," Megan admitted in a deflated tone of voice. "He treats me as if he thinks I'm special, but..." She sighed and lifted her shoulders in a helpless shrug.

"You *are* special," Laura inserted softly.

Megan thanked her mother with a faint heart-breaking smile. "But, other than on the rare occasions when his secretary wasn't in and he asked me to take some dictation in his private office, I've never been alone with him."

"Well, thank goodness for small favors!" Brooke exclaimed.

And, while her heart ached for Megan, Laura fervently, if silently, agreed with Brooke.

"But that doesn't mean he doesn't care for me!" Megan was quick to protest. "Does it, Mother?" she appealed to Laura as she always had.

"No," Laura answered honestly, even though she longed to deny Megan's plea for reassurance. In truth, Laura didn't know what Hank Branson's feelings were.

"Then I'll just hang around until I know how he feels," Megan said with supreme nineteen-year-old optimism. "Now, what do you say we finish up here so we can all go to bed?"

As usual, Laura was the last one to seek her bed later that night. After routinely double-checking the door locks, she turned off the lights behind her before flicking on the muted bedside lamp in her bedroom. It was as she was settling gratefully into her welcoming bed that she remembered one of Hank's remarks with sharp clarity.

I've been alone a long time, Laura.

As the sound of his voice whispered through her mind, Laura felt her skin prickle. Yes, Hank Branson had the look of a man alone. But he also had the look of a man with a sensuous nature. And he had accepted an invitation to attend what he himself had described as traditionally a family holiday gathering. Was there significance in his acceptance of her invitation?

Laura moved restlessly in the bed, which suddenly felt alien to her. She didn't want to pursue this train of thought, yet she could not stop herself. Was Hank perhaps a man tired of being alone? Moreover, was he a man actively seeking a relationship?

A soft gasp escaped Laura's lips, a gasp caused by the intensity of the anticipatory thrill she experienced at the speculation of Hank's motivation. Then she clamped her hand over her mouth to stifle a moan.

Megan!

The very idea of Hank Branson being personally interested in her daughter was so distressing that Laura closed her mind to any further speculation. She was too tired. She didn't want to think about it. She didn't want to think about *him*.

But, deep inside, Laura knew that what she wanted to think about least of all was her own reaction and attraction to Hank Branson.

Two

The Monday after Easter dawned slate gray and chilly. Rain interspersed with the ping of sleet spattered the windows on the west side of the town house. The weather was an almost mirror-perfect reflection of Laura Seaton's mood. In a word, Laura was depressed.

Since it had been close to dawn before Laura finally fell asleep, being awakened shortly after nine on the day after a holiday, when she didn't have to rush off to her shop, did little to lighten her disposition. When she entered the noisy kitchen, she looked as stormy as the dark clouds hanging low in the sky. The chorus of greetings that washed over her stopped Laura in her tracks.

"Good morning, Mother," Megan and Brooke sang in fresh-voiced unison.

"Good morning, Laura." The echo came from her son-in-law, Donald Tobias.

"Morning, Ms. Seaton," Ruth Miller, Laura's housekeeper of thirteen years, called from her position at the stove.

"Bladem glop!" The bright-eyed seven-month-old Heather exclaimed gleefully, banging her spoon against the wooden tray on her high chair.

"Humph," Laura grunted in response.

"Uh-oh," Mcgan said to the room at large. "The tigress is on the prowl this morning."

There were mornings, few in actual number, due to overwork and underrest, when Laura would greet the day with less than enthusiasm. Being normal quick-witted kids, Brooke and Megan had swiftly learned to identify their mother's mood on those rare occasions. While still in junior high school, Megan had made the teasing observation that when Laura was tired or hadn't slept well, she came into the kitchen like a prowling tigress. Both girls had continued to use the comparison through the years.

It was now an established family joke that everyone laughed at, including the baby, who didn't know what she was laughing at but joined in because she was a naturally happy child. Laura was the sole exception to the merriment. Raising her eyes as if beseeching deliverance, she moved into the room on a direct course to the coffeepot.

"She's stalking the coffeepot," Don said in the hushed tones of a TV reporter giving the play-by-play of a tense golf match. "Now she's reaching for the handle, now pouring out the dark brew. Wait, wait, yes, she is lifting the cup to her lips. You know," he said in an aside, "it has been rumored that, when imbibed, the brew has magical properties powerful enough to change the feared tigress into the beautiful and charming Laura Seaton. Will it work?" His voice took on a note of expectation. "We'll soon know, folks. She's sipping...once, twice. Wait a minute, she's glancing up, she's...she's... Holy moly, it is magical! The tigress has been changed into Laura Seaton and...she is smiling!"

"Cute," Laura drawled, but she *was* smiling. She couldn't help herself; her son-in-law's offbeat sense of humor had amused her from the first day Brooke dragged him home to meet "Mother." Brooke had been fifteen and Don nineteen at the time.

"Grafuf!"

Her drawn face softening, Laura turned to smile at her granddaughter. "Good morning to you, too, darling," she said, absently picking up a napkin to smooth away a dab of oatmeal clinging to the tiny chin. "You appear to be enjoying your breakfast."

"And creating quite a mess in the bargain," Don observed dryly, stroking his finger down his daughter's chubby arm.

Gurgling happily, Heather grasped her father's finger with a sticky hand.

"And what about you, Ms. Seaton?" Ruth asked as she came to the table to collect the others' breakfast dishes. "What would you like to eat this morning?"

Laura looked up at the well-endowed woman, who had alternately mothered her and bullied her for thirteen years yet still refused to call her anything but Ms. Seaton. "Oh, Ruth, I don't think I want—"

"You may as well eat, Mother," Megan interrupted to offer advice. "You know you need a shot of protein as well as the caffeine to keep the tigress at bay."

Laura tilted her head to frown at her younger daughter. "Don't you have classes to attend or something?"

Megan grinned. "Mother, you know very well that business school is closed for the Easter holiday until Wednesday."

"Some mothers have all the luck," Laura muttered.

"Meg's right, Mother," Brooke piped in. "You really should eat something."

Sighing deeply, Laura shifted her dark gaze from Megan to Brooke and then to Don. "Don't you have anything to add to this chorus of advice?"

Don nodded sagely. "I can highly recommend the French toast and sausage links."

"Oh, spare me!" Laura groaned. "Good grief. Caffeine, protein and hundreds of calories." Ignoring his grin and the girls' laughter, she looked at Ruth. "Okay, I give up. I'll have one poached egg on..."

"Diet wheat toast," Ruth finished for her.

"Oh, my," Laura moaned to Ruth's retreating back. "How predictable I've become in middle age."

"Middle age!" Megan yelped.

"You?" Brooke cried.

"No way!" Don exclaimed.

"Baloney." Ruth snorted.

"Maazia!" Heather squealed.

"Why, thank you, all." Though Laura's tone was humble with gratitude, her eyes were beginning to glow with their usual brightness, and a teasing smile played over her mouth, telling them without words that the morning tigress had subsided to the darker depths of her personality.

As invariably happened on the occasions when they were together as a family, the kitchen resounded with the noise of everyone talking and laughing at once. The main topic of conversation was a postmortem of Laura's holiday gathering; the consensus being that a good time was had by all.

Laura had long since finished her breakfast and was gently bouncing Heather on her knees when she tossed a question into a lull in the chatter.

"What do you kids have planned for today?"

"I've got to cut out of here pretty soon," Megan answered, her eyes widening in surprise as she glanced at the clock on one wall. "I'm meeting some of the girls from school for lunch and shopping at the mall."

"And we have to leave soon, too," Brooke said, reaching for Heather. "Since I knew we wouldn't be home for the holiday, I invited Don's parents and sister for dinner tonight and, as I decided to serve prime rib, I must get home and get started on the preparations." She frowned at Heather as she began to wiggle fretfully. "I think we'd better get going," she added to her husband, "because this little gal's ready for a nap."

"Right," Don agreed, standing to take the child into his arms. "Come on, pumpkin," he crooned, walking toward the hallway. "Daddy'll get you cleaned up."

Her expression revealing her love for both the man and the child, Brooke trailed after Don, calling, "I'll start packing our stuff."

"And I've got to go," Megan said, jumping up.

"Could you use some money?" Laura asked.

"I could always use money," Meg replied with a grin. "But, no thanks. I'm determined to stay on this new budget I've worked out." She, too, headed for the hallway, adding with a laugh, "But that shouldn't be too tough, considering the generous salary Hank pays me."

Hank. Laura closed her mind against an image of him that was beginning to form. She wasn't ready to think about him or her own confusion regarding him. She needed to be alone to sort out her feelings. Yet, as she had learned to her chagrin the night before, dismissing him from her thoughts entirely was impossible. Hank Branson clung to her memory like a sticky web adhering to a tree branch.

"Will you be home for dinner?" Laura called after Megan, pushing the thought of Hank to the back of her mind.

"I don't know." Megan was shrugging into her coat as she reentered the kitchen. "The girls mentioned taking in a movie after shopping, but nothing definite was settled." She glanced again at the clock, then started for the back door. "Were you planning something special for dinner?" she asked, pausing with her hand on the doorknob to look at Laura with raised eyebrows.

"No." Laura shook her head. "As a matter of fact, since there was so much food left over yesterday, I thought we'd just make do with that."

"Suppose I call you . . . okay?"

"Fine." Laura moved her hand in a shooing wave. "You'd better go or you'll be late."

Knowing too well her mother's insistence on punctuality, Megan grinned and opened the door. "Right. I'm gone. I'll see you when I see you. Bye, Ruth."

Laura and Ruth looked at each other; both winced then laughed as the door slammed.

"I'll know that young lady has grown up the first time she shuts a door without rattling every window in the house," Ruth said in a dry tone.

"Umm," Laura murmured absently, staring at the portal. Her expression was wistful when she transferred her gaze to the housekeeper. "I hope the day doesn't come too soon."

Although Ruth had never known the joys of motherhood, her smile held understanding. "Missing your babies, Ms. Seaton?"

"No... Well, a little, maybe." Laura sighed. "They did seem to grow up rather quickly, didn't they?"

"Too quickly," Ruth agreed. "Why, it hardly seems any time at all since I came to work for you when Brooke and Megan were still little girls." Her smile brightened. "But at least we now have Heather to spoil."

"Yes." Laura laughed. "Isn't it fun?"

"Uh-huh." The older woman chuckled. "And the best part is, when she gets tired and cranky, we can hand her to her mother or father and let them deal with the teething and upset tummies and all the assorted maladies children are prone to."

"And let them walk the floor till all hours of the morning," Laura interjected.

"Right." Ruth nodded vigorously. "You know what?" she added, frowning. "I don't think I am in such an all-fire hurry for Megan to grow up, after all."

"Why not?" Laura raised her eyebrows.

The older woman's chuckle held a rueful note. "Because then she'll be getting married and having babies, and, even though you and I are slightly removed, we can't help getting involved and worried and upset over every childhood complaint, regardless of how insignificant it may be."

"Once a mother, always a mother," Laura quoted her own mother. "I'm getting tired just thinking about it." She did suddenly feel weary, but not from envisioning some future worry over a sick infant. The weariness had struck with the image that had leaped into her mind when Ruth mentioned the inevitability of Megan getting married and having babies of her own. Of course, the image was of a tall earthy-looking man with brown hair tipped with gold and amber eyes that seemed to have the power to pierce the soul.

Laura shuddered; Ruth saw it. "You do look tired," she said. "And it's no wonder, after the way you worked to arrange your *relaxing* holiday dinner. Why don't you go back to bed after Brooke leaves?"

Laura smiled. "You worked every bit as hard as I did to pull the feast together. Are you going back to bed?"

Ruth shook her head. "No, but then, I only worked here, in the house. You're the one wearing yourself to a nub earning the wherewithal to keep it all together."

Laura was not above accepting her housekeeper's praise, nor sharing it. "I couldn't have done it without you, Ruth, not any of it." She grasped the woman's hand impulsively. "I'll never be able to repay you for all you've done to help me these past thirteen years."

Although Ruth snorted in disbelief, she flushed with pleasure and gratitude. "Ms. Seaton, if there's any thanking to be done, I'm the one who should be doing it."

"No, Ruth—" Laura began, but the older woman interrupted.

"Yes," she insisted. "I was forty-four years old, alone and scared when I came to you from the employment agency." Her face looked pinched with the memory. "You not only gave me a job, Ms. Seaton, you gave me a home and a family, which I never really had." Tears glistened in her eyes. "You know there's not a thing in this world I wouldn't do for you."

"I know," Laura murmured, blinking against the sting of tears in her eyes. "And there is something I'd like you to do for me, if you will."

"Name it."

Laura's soft lips curved into a tender smile. "I'd like you to call me Laura."

"But . . . !"

"Please, Ruth," Laura begged over the housekeeper's attempt to protest. "We're friends . . . aren't we?"

Outflanked by kindness, Ruth acknowledged defeat with a shaky laugh. "Yes . . . Laura, we are friends." She arched one eyebrow. "So, would you do a friend a favor?"

"Of course," Laura replied at once.

"Good." Ruth smiled with satisfaction. "As soon as the kids leave, I'd like you to go back to bed."

Laura laughed. "Okay, you win. I promise I'll go directly to bed after the kids leave."

Less than a half hour later, Laura sighed as she slid between the sheets on her unmade bed. Though she wouldn't have admitted it to another soul, she was tired. Due to her exquisite taste and expertise in interior decorating, her services were in constant demand, and she had been working at a breakneck pace to keep up with her clientele.

Laura's bank balance gave more than ample proof of how financially rewarding her efforts were. The praise heaped upon her by her clients was rewarding, yet the price was high in terms of the physical wear and tear. Laura sorely needed rest.

Snuggling into a warm cocoon of comfort, Laura yawned and shut her eyes. The vision that instantly commanded her mind and attention held slumber at bay. Sighing, she faced her dilemma.

What to do about Hank Branson?

The question was academic, and Laura knew it. What could she do about Hank Branson? Placing the blame for the chill that shivered through her on the low growl of thunder rumbling in the west, Laura curled into a ball and drew the covers more tightly around her trembling body.

She didn't want to think about Hank Branson. She didn't want to think, period. Laura wanted to sleep. The image clarifying behind her eyelids made it too clear that her subconscious didn't particularly care what she wanted.

In the image, amber eyes appeared to mock Laura's desperate attempt to escape into unconsciousness. An enticing male mouth curved into a sensuous smile. Though the experience was new, the effects of Hank's smile were already familiar to Laura; she had suffered from those effects from the instant she'd glanced up to find him watching her—was it less than twenty-four hours ago?

To Laura, tired and susceptible, it seemed like forever since Hank's eyes and smile had begun haunting her.

Hank.

Merely thinking his name brought a groan to her lips and an ache to the very core of her body. Even as Laura denied the ache, it spread insidiously, causing a tremor in her midsection. An emptiness yawned deep inside, almost painful in intensity. She wanted, needed . . .

"Ridiculous!" Laura exclaimed aloud as her eyes flew wide open. It had been years since her body had made *that* kind of demand! As to that, she had never been an overly sensuous or passionate woman. Yet, now, passion was sweeping through her with gathering force, arousing every nuance of sensuality within her. It wasn't merely ridiculous; it was astonishing! What had happened to her?

Hank Branson! Although the answer to her silent question shocked Laura's sensibilities, it excited her senses. Her heart pounded; her nerves twanged; her blood raced. Her lips tingled from a deep-seated yearning to test and taste the warmth and texture of his masculine mouth.

And, as if all the symptoms of physical starvation she was enduring were not enough, Laura was plagued by the incredible feeling that she belonged with him— to him!

Beginning to panic because of the strength of the feminine phenomenon unfurling inside her, Laura raked her mind for an explanation of her extraordinary response to a man who was little more than a stranger to her.

Midlife crisis? Laura pondered the excuse. From the little she had read and heard about the traumatic condition, she couldn't decide if the way she was feeling was symptomatic or not, but she strongly suspected that it wasn't.

No, in truth, Laura secretly suspected that the malady she suffered from was the plain old garden-variety type of physical attraction to a particularly magnetic member of the opposite sex.

Identifying and facing the cause of her discontent didn't alleviate Laura's confusion. It had been a long time since she'd experienced the heady flow of passion, and even when she had, she'd never felt anything remotely like the hot heavy immediacy that had splintered through her the moment she'd glanced up to see his glittering amber eyes. And, rather than subside, the feeling intensified every time his audacious image invaded her mind.

It was odd—no!—it was darn weird. Hank Branson was a man, like other men, Laura chided herself. Well, perhaps not quite like other men, she conceded in the next instant. But why wasn't he like other men? she cried in mute frustration. In what way was Hank different?

Giving up all hope of sleep for the moment, Laura concentrated on the enticing vision of her tormentor in an effort to determine exactly what it was about him that set Hank apart from other men.

Laura ticked off his attribute: so his visage had the advantage of sharply defined and sculptured features; so his masculine form was constructed of an angular long-boned frame laced with corded, finely honed muscles; so his gold-tipped unruly hair had a crisp healthy sheen. Taking all those factors into consideration, why should Hank be put in a class all by himself?

Laura groaned aloud. A man very much like other men? Not likely! At least, not any other man she had ever had the misfortune to innocently invite into her home, or any man she had ever met outside of her home, either.

But what was Hank Branson really like? What made him tick? How did he think?

For answers to her nagging questions, Laura had only one point of reference: her daughter, Megan.

In connection to Megan's employment, Laura knew one fact about Hank. He was willing to give inexperienced people a chance to prove themselves.

The previous fall Megan had been hired as a part-time clerical employee by Branson Construction Company. At the time she had explained to Laura that the owner, Hank Branson, routinely hired young people who had been referred to him by the secretarial school Megan was attending.

Throughout the fall and winter, Megan had discussed her work and her employer in increasingly glowing terms—most especially her employer. Now, on a miserable spring morning, Laura tried to recall everything Megan had told her about Hank during those conversations.

Since Laura had been distracted by the demands of her own growing business, her memory was sketchy, at best. She vaguely remembered Megan praising her boss for his demand for quality in all phases of his business, and for his fair, if sometimes gruff, treatment of his employees. But, for Laura, the single most important bit of information Megan had reported about him was that Hank Branson was—amazingly, in Megan's opinion—a dedicated bachelor.

Hank was unmarried.

The knowledge shouldn't have affected Laura one way or another, yet it did, and she knew it. She had met him the day before, and he was a virtual stranger to her, and still Laura felt relief shiver through her.

Suddenly impatient—with herself, with the baffling reaction she was feeling to him as a man, and with the persistent image of Hank that was entrenched in her mind—Laura compressed her mouth with grim determination.

Other than for Megan's sake, because the girl was obviously infatuated with him, Hank Branson meant nothing to her, Laura assured herself as she settled more comfortably beneath the covers. There was no reason for her to even see the man again.

As for her daughter, Laura mused, Megan was obviously in the throes of a large case of hero worship, which would die a natural death with the very next attractive man who caught her teenager's fancy.

If nothing else, Laura told herself with a spark of amusement, the quickening of response she felt reaffirmed her femininity. But she didn't have time in her life for a man, not even for the vision of one. She was tired, thus vulnerable. All that was required for her to get her head back together was some rest. Clinging to the thought, Laura finally banished Hank's image by concentrating for all she was worth on mentally reviewing the financial records she needed to prepare before filing her income tax report. The exercise never failed to lull her into sleep. Laura's last coherent thought before her consciousness surrendered was a reiteration of an earlier conclusion.

There was no reason whatever for her to see the man again.

Laura breezed into her shop the next morning looking ten years younger. She had slept soundly, her slumber interrupted for only a few hours when Ruth woke her for dinner. Megan had called to say she'd be eating out, and Laura had stayed awake until the girl was home, and then had gone back to bed. And, since the image of her tormentor had not returned to haunt her, Laura decided with satisfaction that the unusual physical attraction she had experienced for Hank Branson had faded into the realm of speculation...where it belonged.

Relief lent a spring to her brisk stride. When Laura entered the spacious office located behind the showroom, a smile lighted her sparkling hazel eyes as her glance came to rest on the elegant form of her assistant.

"Good morning, Ginnie," she said brightly. "Did you have a pleasant holiday visit with your family?"

The vivacious twenty-six-year-old redhead flashed her a dazzling smile. "I had a terrific time," Ginnie Devlon replied in the smoky voice that guaranteed immediate attention from most women and every man. "All six of us—with assorted spouses and offspring—converged on the homestead. It was absolute bedlam." She laughed softly. "My parents loved every minute of it."

Having had the opportunity to meet Ginnie's family en masse, Laura laughed with her. The fifth of six children, Ginnie had three brothers and two sisters, all of whom shared her tall lithe figure, startling good looks, flaming hair and quick, sometimes acerbic wit, which, when together, they honed on one another. From observation, Laura knew their family gatherings were far from quiet and never dull. Amazingly, Ginnie's parents were rather subdued yet appeared to bask in the brilliance of their children's sharp intelligence and high spirits.

"How did your party fare?"

Laura nearly lost her smile in reaction to a brief flashing image of a tall man with glittering amber eyes. "As usual," she answered, fully aware of exactly how unusual the day had turned out for her. "The food was excellent."

Ginnie gave her a rakish grin. "I can't imagine a solitary thing not being excellent for one of your soirees—it wouldn't dare!"

Though her lips twitched, Laura controlled the urge to return the grin. Considering the thought, planning and expense she always poured into her parties, Laura felt justified in expecting everything to be excellent.

"I work at it," Laura said with simple honesty.

"As you do everything you turn your mind to," Ginnie observed dryly, sending a telling glance to the thick client folders piled on her own and Laura's desks.

Laura allowed the twitch at her lips to grow into a satisfied smile. "It's been worth the work, though, hasn't it? Business is flourishing."

"Flourishing!" Ginnie's entrancing laughter danced like sunlight in the room. "I'd say it's more like overwhelming! There are days I'm not sure if I'm coming, going or already long gone!"

"But you love it," Laura said, "every bit as much as I do myself."

"Yes, I do," the redhead confessed with a grin. Rising with feline grace, Ginnie walked to the tiny kitchenette Laura had had installed in the far corner of the room. "Ready for coffee?" she called over her shoulder, her grin spreading as she witnessed her boss grimace as she seated herself at her desk and flipped open the account books.

"Uh-huh, thank you," Laura responded in a distracted tone. She was already immersed in the dreaded figures she was preparing for her accountant.

Her movements swift and economical, Ginnie prepared the coffee then set a steaming mug close to her employer's hand. Laura acknowledged the small act of service with another murmur of thanks.

Within minutes both women were immersed in their work, Laura to the extent that she heard Ginnie conversing on the telephone with clients but was hardly aware of what the younger woman was saying. But then, she didn't have to be aware of Ginnie's every professional conversation. Ginnie was long past the point of requiring Laura's counsel in connection to her work.

Hours later Laura was still struggling through the quagmire of figures when the phone rang again. As with the numerous earlier calls, Laura barely registered the sound of Ginnie's low-pitched voice, nor did she notice the edge of exasperation that slowly crept into her tone.

"Laura?" Though soft, Ginnie's voice caught Laura's attention.

"Umm?" The direct call shattered her concentration. Frowning, Laura glanced at the younger woman.

Holding one palm over the mouthpiece of the receiver, Ginnie lifted her shoulders in a helpless shrug. "It's a Mr. Branson, and the gentleman insists on speaking to you."

Hank? Laura's mind went blank; her pulse went crazy. Why would Hank be calling her? Even as the question formed, Laura was determinedly squashing a thrill of anticipation. Keeping her voice cool and detached was not the easiest thing Laura had ever done.

"Insists?"

"Adamantly," Ginnie said, nodding. "I told him you were extremely busy." She grimaced at the receiver. "He said that he was just as busy and wasn't planning on taking up much of your time." Her expression was wry. "He has a sexy voice but..." She shrugged once more.

Laura understood perfectly. She had not only met the man, she had heard Megan describe him. She could imagine the impatience Ginnie had heard in his tone.

"Will you speak to him?" Ginnie narrowed her leaf-green eyes in a manner that was familiar to Laura. Without words, the younger woman was telling her employer that she'd be delighted to educate the sexy-voiced but imperious-sounding man.

A faint smile curving her lips, Laura reached for her own phone. Drawing a slow calming breath, she lifted the receiver to her ear. Her cool voice didn't reveal the tremulous excitement she was experiencing. "What can I do for you, Mr. Branson?"

Three

You can begin by calling me Hank . . . Laura.''

His dry chiding tone reactivated the thrill of anticipation fluttering inside Laura. Steeling herself against it, and him, she injected a note of impatience into her voice. ''All right. What can I do for you . . . Hank?''

''Hmm, it is a chilly spring,'' he drawled. ''I could almost feel the frost in your secretary's voice.''

''My assistant,'' Laura said.

''Whatever.'' Hank's tone dismissed the other woman. ''I called to set up an appointment with you,'' he went on.

Laura frowned. ''An appointment for what?'' she asked in confusion.

''What business are you in?'' Hank answered with a question.

''You want to hire an interior decorator?''

"Right in one." Hank's voice contained patient amusement. "I've decided to have the sample home in the subdivision decorated before opening it for public view," he explained. "And, since Megan works for me, I naturally thought of you first. Would you be interested?"

Interested? Laura bit down on her lip. She was entirely too interested. Her first impulse was to tell him she was too busy, too booked up, too anything. Her good business sense saved her from tossing away the opportunity to establish herself in a different and, for her, as yet untapped area of the decorating scene.

"Yes, of course I'm interested," she finally replied.

"Good... but, there is one small hitch."

Wasn't there always? Laura sighed. "What is that?"

"We're pressed for time," Hank said. "I had wanted to open the sample home at the end of the month. Could you pull it off that quickly?"

"No," Laura answered without hesitation. A shiver trickled down her spine at the sound of his soft, appreciative and far too sexy laugh.

"I do like a decisive woman," Hank murmured. When he spoke again, his voice was brisk. "Can you give me a ballpark figure of how long it will take?"

"Not before seeing the project and knowing the extent of the work involved," Laura replied just as briskly. Once again his low laugh tickled her ear—which suddenly seemed directly connected to her spine.

"Okay, we'll get together," he returned. "Do you have any free time tomorrow to come out to the site and look over the house?"

Tomorrow! Laura felt a flutter of panic; she didn't know exactly why she felt it, but she definitely felt it. The even tone of voice she managed amazed her. "If you will hold on a moment, I'll check my schedule."

"Certainly."

Laura barely heard Hank's prompt response—she was too busy asking herself if she had left her brain in bed that morning. Not twenty-four hours ago, she had decided it would be best if she didn't see him again. She didn't need the complication of a man in her life, most particularly the man her daughter was obviously infatuated with. Yet, here she was checking her schedule for a free moment to meet with him!

Shaking her head in wonder, Laura glanced around, as if searching for a place to hide. A contemplative smile eased the tension around her mouth as her gaze came to rest on Ginnie's openly curious expression. Feeling the panic subside, Laura slid her palm over the receiver.

"What do you have on for tomorrow?" she asked the younger woman in a quiet tone.

Ginnie didn't bother looking at her appointment book. "I have a meeting with Jennie Dobbins at one," she answered. "Why, would you like me to field this one for you?"

"Yes." Laura mouthed the word while sliding her palm from the receiver. "Would ten-thirty be suitable, Hank?" She raised her eyebrows at Ginnie, who nodded.

"Eleven-thirty would be better," he replied.

"Eleven-thirty?" Laura repeated for Ginnie's benefit. The other woman gave a quick nod, and Laura went on smoothly. "Yes, that will be all right."

"Good." Hank went on to give her directions to the subdivision, which Laura carefully jotted down in her notepad, and finished by saying, "I'll meet you at the sample home...okay?"

"Yes." Laura had a hard time keeping the satisfaction from her voice. "Goodbye, Hank."

Laura's satisfaction with her clever manipulation in agreeing to take on the job of decorating Hank's sample home while maintaining a personal distance from the disturbing man, was of short duration.

As the long hours of the afternoon wore into the equally long hours of evening, a sensation of yawning emptiness swallowed Laura's contentment. Yet, unwilling to examine the empty feeling, let alone define it, she buried it under the mound of figures in her account books, both in the office throughout the afternoon and in her small study in the town house later that evening.

By the time she collapsed into bed that night, not only were her record books ready for her accountant, Laura's mind was so numbed by figures that she fell into a deep sleep, undisturbed by dreams of a tall sexy-voiced man.

Laura's determination to avoid contact with Hank was sorely tried by her first look at Ginnie the next morning. The weather, which had been damp and chilly, made a capricious spring turnabout. Butter-yellow sunlight poured its warmth into the earth, which had been parched by winter, and the illusive scent from the bursting spring flowers was in the air.

Dressed for the season, Ginnie resembled a delicate early bloom.

Vaguely disgruntled, Laura felt her spirits plummet as she ran a comprehensive and disheartening gaze over the younger woman's elegant form. Unbound, Ginnie's thick mane fell in smooth shimmering waves to the middle of her back, where the dark red strands should have clashed with the hot pink of her suit jacket, yet strangely did not. The severe tailoring of the paler pink silk shirt she was wearing under the jacket merely emphasized her feminine attributes. Her high-heeled patent leather pumps complemented her long slender legs and delicate ankles. Her expertly applied makeup highlighted and deepened the green of her exotic eyes.

Although always attired impeccably, Laura felt decidedly dowdy by comparison. Imagining the impact her gorgeous assistant would have on the virile man she would soon be meeting, Laura repressed a sigh and waved Ginnie on her way as the woman breezed out of the showroom at eleven o'clock. And, for at least fifteen minutes after she left, Laura feared she might drown in the lingering scent of Ginnie's tantalizing perfume.

The tinkling sound of the tiny bell attached to the showroom door sent out its jingling warning of the presence of a prospective customer, and, as Laura rose from her desk and walked into the room, she recognized a particularly fussy client. With a quick glance at her wristwatch, she noted the time. Ginnie would be meeting Hank within a few minutes. Swallowing a groan, Laura formed her lips into a warm welcoming smile. It was going to be a very long day.

* * *

The cellular phone rang in the panel van just as Hank opened the door on the driver's side. Sliding behind the wheel, he grasped the receiver and shot a look at the dashboard clock. It was exactly 11:28. Apparently Laura was both decisive and punctual. Smiling with satisfaction, he depressed the Speak button.

"Branson," Hank identified himself bluntly.

"Hank, there's a woman here to see you," came the voice of the job foreman. "She's waiting at the sample."

Hank flicked the key in the ignition, firing the van. "Right. I'm on my way. Give the lady a cup of coffee." He was replacing the receiver when he heard the reply.

"Will do."

The first thing Hank noticed as he strode into the sample house was the hot pink of her suit. A smile twitched his sculpted mouth. The second thing he noticed was the gleaming mass of flaming red hair. Hank's lips thinned and compressed.

Hearing the thud of his work boots on the bare wood floor, the woman turned to face him. Her mouth curved into a professional smile.

"Mr. Branson?" She started toward him, long slender hand extended.

Hank's eyes narrowed as he clasped her soft hand. Without doubt, she was a strikingly beautiful woman...but she was the wrong beautiful woman. Anger flared through Hank. He concealed it well.

"Ms...?" He arched his dark brows questioningly.

"Devlon," she supplied in the low, attractively husky voice Hank recognized from the phone the day before. "Ginnie Devlon. I'm Laura's assistant."

"I see." As he released her hand, Hank made a swift expert perusal of her from her mane of red hair to the shiny tips of her patent leather shoes. Being wholly male and as healthy as a war-horse, Hank could appreciate and admire Ginnie Devlon's appeal; in her bright spring outfit, she embodied any man's image of a delectably wrapped package of feminine allure. Any man but Hank, that is. He simply wasn't interested. His lack of response was clear in his brusque tone of voice. "I was expecting your employer."

"Yes, I know, but—" Ginnie began. Hank cut her off without compunction.

"Then why isn't she here?"

"Laura is very busy at this time," Ginnie explained, seemingly unruffled by his abrupt rudeness. "She thought I could handle this assignment for her."

"She thought wrong," Hank retorted, allowing some of the anger searing through him to surface. "I don't mean to be insulting, Ms. Devlon, but I'm also very busy." His smile strained, Hank escorted her outside. "You'll have to excuse me. I have a pressing appointment."

Ginnie's expression betrayed her astonishment. "But, Mr. Branson! What about the—"

Hank shut out the sound of the woman's voice by climbing into the van and slamming the door behind him. A moment later the vehicle shot away from the house, leaving a plume of dust in its wake.

"Women!" Hank wasn't even aware of growling the word aloud. He was mad, damn mad. And as he recalled the thrill of anticipation he had felt at increasingly regular intervals ever since he'd made the appointment with Laura, he became madder still.

Haunted by his memories of her lovely face, her soft voice, her bright hazel eyes and her slender, maturely rounded body, Hank had barely slept the night before. In his restlessness, his mind had tortured his body by conjuring images of Laura so erotic he had spent the long dark hours writhing in his own sweat. By dawn, Hank was a solid mass of expectation. He yearned to touch her, hold her, taste her, but, knowing he'd be denied that pleasure, he'd content himself with seeing her, talking to her, being with her.

And Laura had sent him Ginnie Devlon. Hank gritted his teeth in frustration. He felt cheated; he didn't like the feeling one damn bit.

How dare she make an appointment with him then send an assistant in her stead? Hank railed, gripping the steering wheel as though he'd take extreme pleasure from tearing it from its column. Did Laura believe him to be a hormone-driven boy to be appeased by a pretty face? Hank's palm slapped the gear stick as he downshifted viciously. Well, for a thirty-nine-year-old woman and a grandmother to boot, Laura Seaton apparently hadn't learned much about men in general...and Hank Branson in particular, he derided in silent rage. But she was about to receive a thorough education on the subject, Hank assured himself. And he was going to love playing teacher.

* * *

Laura was reaching for the ringing phone when she heard the melodic tinkle of the tiny bell, signaling the departure of her demanding customer. The supercilious woman had been in the showroom some thirty-odd minutes. Laura had kept her surface composure throughout, while inside she felt like exploding.

As she grabbed the receiver from its cradle, Laura was not in the best of all possible moods. Her inner turmoil was reflected in her voice by a slightly clipped edge as she intoned the name of her business in her usual professional greeting.

"New Design. May I help you?" As she spoke into the receiver, Laura experienced a strange prickling sensation at the back of her neck, not unlike the feeling one got when being intently stared at. Frowning, she began to turn, but stopped abruptly at the exasperated sound of her assistant's normally calm low-pitched voice.

"Laura, I ran into a wall."

Alarm raced through Laura as she imagined Ginnie's flashy little car, the front end crumpled like an accordion against a retaining wall.

"Good Lord! Ginnie, are you all right?"

"Oh, I'm fine," Ginnie drawled. "Except for a few bruises to my ego."

Ego? Laura blinked in confusion. The woman sounded much too wry, too calm. Was she in shock? "Ginnie," Laura said in a soothing tone. "Where did this happen? What wall did you run into?"

"It happened at the subdivision," Ginnie replied. "And the wall's name was Branson."

"Hank?"

"Hank."

Startled by the grim sound of the voice from behind her, Laura jolted around to stare in baffled astonishment at the tall man standing in the office doorway. At the sight of him, a funny thrill—a combination of trepidation and excitement—shivered through her body. Dressed in tan cotton pants and shirt, both of which were sprinkled with a fine coating of dust, and with a smudge of dirt defining one high cheekbone, he was still the best-looking male Laura had ever had the misfortune to be disrupted by.

One sturdy work boot crossed negligently over the other, bared forearms folded across his chest, Hank Branson was leaning against the door frame. Laura was not deceived by his indolent pose. One glance at his eyes was all that was necessary to dispel the picture of ease he presented.

Hank was piercing her with 'the look' from his glittering amber eyes.

"Wh-what..." Laura's throat felt parched, and her senses were so rattled she was unaware of the muffled sounds issuing from the receiver she still clutched in one hand until Hank inclined his head, drawing her attention to it.

"Say goodbye to Ms. Devlon," he instructed with soft but unmistakable command.

Ginnie! Laura lifted the receiver. "Ginnie, I'm sorry," she apologized contritely.

"What is going on there?" Ginnie demanded. "Do I hear a man's voice?"

Laura moistened her dry lips with the tip of her tongue and had to compress a shudder caused by the intensity of the gaze that followed the action. "Yes...ah, I...can't talk now." Struck by her own understatement, Laura swallowed a burst of nervous laughter. "Mr. Branson is here. I'll have to explain everything later."

"Hank Branson is in the office with you?" Ginnie exclaimed. "Now?"

"Yes, I..."

"Say goodbye, Laura." This time, Hank's command was laced with steel.

Though she was tempted, Laura prudently decided not to test him. She gave him a withering look but obeyed his order just the same. "I must hang up, Ginnie. I'll talk to you later this afternoon."

"Don't make book on it," Hank murmured.

"But..." Ginnie began in protest.

Laura gently returned the receiver to the cradle, then raised her chin and glared at him. "Now, what is your complaint, Mis-ter Branson?" she asked succinctly.

Hank cocked an eyebrow. "We—meaning you and I—had an appointment this morning." His soft voice took on a chiding tone. "You failed to keep our appointment, Laura. So I'm here to collect you."

Collect? Collect! Laura's slender form shook from the rush of anger that swept through her. She would not be treated like a tardy child who required collecting! It took every ounce of dignity she possessed to refrain from shouting at him.

"You requested the expertise of an experienced decorator. I sent you one of the best!"

"I want you."

Laura went absolutely still, helpless against the molten heat that surged through her at Hank's grittily voiced demand. Telling herself that he was demanding the services of her talent as a decorator, not her personally, didn't help very much. Images, fleeting but erotically detailed, flashed through her mind. Images of herself and Hank, their naked bodies entwined in wild sensuous abandonment....

One particularly clear image of Hank's hard-looking mouth, open and moving hungrily over her bare skin, sent chills leapfrogging down her spine and set her pulses hammering. Consumed by a sudden clawing desire like nothing she had ever experienced or even dreamed of, Laura was reduced to staring at him in mute appeal.

A tightness grasped her throat when Hank pushed himself away from the door frame. Her throat worked, but no sound issued from her lips as he sauntered toward her. Apprehensive excitement churned inside her as he raised one arm with apparent lazy indifference. Mesmerized by the strength of the attraction she felt for him and the measured slowness of his movements, Laura was unprepared for his sudden swift action.

Before she knew what was happening, Hank had plucked her navy-blue white-pin-striped suit jacket from its hanger on the coat rack in the corner, scooped her handbag and briefcase from her desktop and, grasping her upper arm, began leading her from the office and through the showroom.

"Where...why...? Hank!" Laura dug in her heels two feet from the front door. "What do you think you're doing?" She tried to glare at him but only managed to emit a gasped "Oh!" when he yanked the door open and pulled her through it.

"I'm hurrying you along to your appointment." Hank shot a glance at his wristwatch. "You're already over half an hour late." Serenely ignoring her sputtering attempt at protest, he flicked one hand at the door. "Don't you want to lock up?"

"I want to call the police and have *you* locked up!" Laura exclaimed in a rare burst of temper. "You can't just barge into my shop and drag me away!"

Hank's mouth curved into a devastatingly wicked smile; one dark eyebrow inched into a satanic arch, and the devil danced in his amber eyes. "Wanna bet?"

Laura knew there was no way she could win. She had two choices, neither of which held much appeal. She could either give in gracefully and accompany him to the subdivision, or she could make an absolute fool out of herself by continuing to argue with him in public there on the sidewalk. With a sigh of exasperation, Laura opted for giving in gracefully.

Her state of grace lasted until he opened the door for her on the passenger side of the van. Eyeing the dusty interior Laura shook her head and stepped back. "I am not getting in there," she said flatly.

Hank immediately proved he wasn't slow on the uptake. "I see what you mean," he said, glancing from the grimy van to her crisp neat suit skirt and white silk shirt. A frown puckered his brow as he transferred his gaze to his own liberally dusted clothing. "And I couldn't blame you if you objected to me crawling into your car."

"Oh, for heaven's sake!" Laura exclaimed impatiently. "I have no objections at all to having you in my car! The point is, if you ride with me, you'd have to return later for your van. I'd better follow you to the building site."

His hesitation was brief, but telling. Hank pinned her with an amber stare. "Can I trust you to follow me?"

Anywhere.

The instantaneous response sprang into Laura's mind, then it seemed as though it shivered through the entire length of her body. The connotations contained within the single thought were so unsettling, she went totally blank for a moment.

"Laura?" Hank prompted in a suspicious tone when she failed to reply.

"What?" Laura started, then stammered. "Oh...yes. Ah, of course I'll follow you!"

"Umm." Hank looked unconvinced.

Telling herself to act her age, Laura pulled herself together. "I said I'd follow you, Hank."

His skeptical expression eased, and he nodded acceptance of her word. "Where's your car?"

"You parked in front of it." She indicated a maroon Buick with a wave of her hand.

"Nice," Hank murmured, running an appreciative glance over the gleaming vehicle.

"Thank you."

"You're welcome." Hank's eyes were bright with amusement when he returned his gaze to hers. "Can we go now?"

Laura gave him an arch look. "May I have my jacket, purse and briefcase...or are you holding them for security?"

Laughing, Hank handed the articles to her. "I don't need the security. I trust you," he said. "But I expect to see that pretty car every time I glance into my rearview mirror."

Laura was careful to keep a distance of no more than thirty feet behind the van all the way to the subdivision.

Expecting the usual development of clonelike houses set on miniscule lots, Laura was pleasantly surprised by the uniqueness of Hank's subdivision. The design of every house was not only different but innovative, the lots were spacious and, though still in a rough state of construction, she could imagine how attractive the subdivision would be when the project was finished and the grounds landscaped.

She fell in love with the model home the minute she stepped into the roomy entrance foyer. The feeling increased as Hank ushered her slowly from one large room to another. The structure contained every element Laura had longed for in her own home. The clever placement of an abundance of windows enhanced not the illusion of space but genuine spaciousness. The enormous living room soared up to a glass-paneled cathedral ceiling. A broad open staircase curved majestically to the second story. The master bedroom contained its own bath and dressing room, both of which were only slightly smaller than Laura's bedroom in the town house.

"Well, what do you think?" Hank asked as they descended the stairs. "Do you want to take on the job of decorating it?"

"I'd give my eyeteeth to decorate it," she admitted without hesitation.

Coming to a halt near the base of the stairs, Hank turned to stare at her. He was one step below her; she still had to look up to meet his amber eyes. "When can you begin?" he asked, the corners of his eyes crinkling as a slow melting smile worked its way over his mouth and into her heart.

Laura laughed. "I began the instant I walked through the doorway." She raised her hand to press gently against his chest. The hard warmth that met her fingers sent a chill to the nape of her neck. "If you'll give me some room," she said unsteadily, "I'd like to get started."

"Must I?" His voice was low.

"What?" Hers was almost nonexistent.

"Move."

"Why?"

"I don't want to."

"Why not?"

"I like standing this close to you."

"Oh." Laura's senses swam.

"May I kiss you?" Hank slowly lowered his head.

"Must you?" Laura slowly raised her chin.

"I think so." His breath misted her lips.

"Then I guess you'd better." Her eyelashes slowly lowered.

"Do you want it?" His mouth brushed hers.

"Oh, yes." Laura's mind shut down.

In an empty house, on an open staircase, Laura was kissed as she had never been kissed before. Hank's mouth was hard and gentle, demanding and pleading, warm with tenderness and hot with passion. His arms slipped around her, drawing her into the heat radiating from his strong body. Her breasts were crushed against the hard muscled wall of his chest.

Feelings, sensations, impressions swirled around and through her. She wanted, she needed, she ached for everything that was Hank. It was too much, too arousing, and altogether too soon. A murmur and a slight pressure of her fingertips to his chest were all that was required to end the kiss.

Hank's breathing was ragged and harsh sounding when he raised his head. His eyes were closed; his features were strained. Exhaling roughly, he brought his lips to her forehead. When he spoke, his voice held a disbelieving note of awe.

"Hold on, Nellie, I think the ship's sinking."

He didn't have to elaborate; Laura understood perfectly. She was feeling a similar sensation of drowning. There was a thundering noise in her ears. As her breathing calmed, she identified the sound of her own and Hank's pounding heartbeats. She realized, vaguely, that she should be doing something. She just couldn't remember what that something was.

"Where were we?" she asked absently. A shiver tiptoed down her spine as his lips moved against the overwarm skin of her brow.

"Damned if I know."

"You're not much help."

Hank laughed and tightened his hold on her. Crushed to him, Laura could feel him speak before she heard his words. "It's pretty difficult to help someone else when you haven't one idea on how to go about saving yourself."

His amusement sparked her own. "Poor dear. Do you feel you need saving?"

He loosened his arms and leaned back to stare into her eyes. A crooked smile tilted his attractive mouth. "Saving? No." His eyes glittered with a teasing light. "I'd tell you exactly what I need, but I don't want to scare you off."

Laura's amusement dissolved in a flood of embarrassed excitement. And, though she hadn't blushed for nearly twenty years, she felt warm color flare beneath her skin from her shoulders to her cheeks. "Hank...I...ah..." She had to pause to clear her throat.

"I know." His expression resigned, Hank put some distance between them by backing down the two remaining steps to the base of the staircase in the foyer. "This is all happening too soon for you, isn't it?"

As slight as the separation was, it was enough to allow Laura to breathe more naturally. "Yes," she admitted frankly. "We really don't know each other...do we?"

"Maybe not," he conceded. "But we do know one vital fact about each other."

The leap at every pulse point in her body gave Laura the answer. She asked the question anyway. "And that is?"

"We turn each other on something fierce," he said bluntly. "Don't we?"

Laura suddenly felt young and gauche and inadequate. Too many years had slipped by since she had experienced as much as a glimmer of the passion Hank had so effortlessly aroused within her. She didn't know how to reply to his assertion and so, lowering her eyes, she remained flushed and silent.

"Laura?" The soft entreaty in his voice drew her reluctant gaze up to his darkened eyes.

"Yes?"

"Have I made you feel uncomfortable?"

"Yes," she breathed in admission.

"Would you like me to make myself scarce for a while?"

Hank's understanding and sensitivity drained the flood of heat from her face to settle in a pool surrounding her heart. Her throat was dry; her eyes were moist. "I . . . really should get on with the job you brought me here for," she said.

"Okay." He strode to the door and opened it. But before crossing the threshold, he shattered the illusion of sensitivity by turning to flash a wicked smile at her and murmur a heart-stopping warning. "I'll be back."

Four

Laura stared in blank wonder at the closed door for long minutes after Hank delivered his exit line. Then she laughed. Then she sighed. Then she got to work. It was always easier for her to resolve a problem by literally working it through—and she considered her response to Hank a definite problem.

What was happening to her?

Laura worried the question as she visualized a tall indoor tree standing on the flagstone flooring to one side of the staircase.

A palm tree perhaps? She shook her head, rejecting the idea as too exotic. Hank wasn't in the least exotic looking. He was earthy, magnetic and wholly masculine. No palm tree for Hank. A whimsical smile played over her kiss-softened mouth when another consideration popped into her head. Hank had also revealed a prickly side of his nature when he had stormed into her showroom to collect her. Laura snapped her fingers as inspiration struck. A large tough-looking cactus, of course!

The question of the entranceway answered, she ambled into the spacious living room, a frown tugging her eyebrows together as she concentrated on her emotional condition.

What *had* happened to her?

Try as she would, Laura could come up with only one answer to the query. *Hank Branson had happened to her.* Hank of the shaggy hair and the riveting eyes and the devastating mouth. Hank had walked into her house by invitation... and into her imagination by design. And not for an instant did Laura delude herself about Hank's designs. The kiss he had given her, the kiss they had shared, was by itself an explanation. In the most basic definition of the word, Hank wanted her.

Laura felt both thrilled and alarmed—thrilled because a man like Hank wanted her, and alarmed because she was afraid that she wanted him.

Megan wanted him, too.

Imagining her daughter in an intimate situation with Hank brought a gasp of denial to Laura's lips. Hank was too old for Megan, too mature, too... too much man for the nineteen-year-old girl. And, reasons aside, Laura was forced to admit that she did want him for herself.

The self-acknowledgment was more than enlightening for her; it was mind-blowing.

Standing stock-still in a beautiful but empty room, Laura stared outward into space and inward into herself.

Incredible! It had been years since she had felt even the mildest interest in a man, any man. In fact, the last time... Laura shook her head. She didn't want to recall the last man she had so briefly dated. Still, the memory insisted on being revived.

It was over five years ago. At the time, Laura had been going through a particularly rough period of her life. Her daughters were growing up, and she was working hard and was tired and lonely for something, someone. Against her better judgment, she had agreed to join some friends for drinks at the latest "in" place in the community. Laura had been so out of touch with the current social scene, she'd had no idea the place was a singles' bar. In her innocence, she had assumed the bar was merely the newest watering hole to catch the fancy of the local residents.

Less than fifteen minutes after she'd joined her friends in the dimly lighted bar, a man approached their table. With what Laura later found out was practiced ease, the man introduced himself, then, after chatting for a few minutes, allowed himself to be talked into joining their group of four at the table. He quickly proved to be suave, urbane, reasonably attractive and a good conversationalist. The following day he had called Laura to invite her to dinner. After a brief hesitation, she accepted his invitation. He was ten years older than Laura, recently divorced and utterly charming. He was also on the make, a fact Laura didn't discover until their second date.

A shudder coursed through Laura with the memory of the struggle she'd had escaping unscathed from him that night, and the anger he had unleashed when she adamantly refused to reimburse him with her body for the cost of the two dinners. Her mind flinched from the echo of his disgusted voice, snarling at her, condemning her for being out of touch with the reality of the prevailing mores.

Then and there Laura had decided that if prevailing mores demanded she go to bed with any man who bought her a meal, she'd dine alone and pay the check herself. She had stood firm on her decision ever since.

But Hank hadn't even offered her dinner; he had offered his mouth and the stirring heat of his embrace.

Laura's reverie was shattered by the intense wave of desire that crashed through her. As she absorbed her reflexive sensation to the mere thought of Hank, a self-mocking smile curved her trembling lips. For, in that instant, Laura knew she would accept his as yet unspoken offer... with or without the added attraction of dinner.

The resolve to grant whatever Hank wanted of her was uncharacteristic of Laura, but then, she wasn't feeling at all like herself. In contrast to her normal cool, levelheaded mature personality, she was feeling flustered, unsure and as young as her own daughters.

Experiencing an inner glow from the awakening of something long dormant deep inside her, Laura smiled and glanced around the bare room. A shiver of anticipation tingled down her spine. Without being told, she knew that Hank had designed the house. It was exactly like him—big, open, warm and yet austere. The realization of the parallels between him and the house galvanized her into action.

Spinning around, Laura strode to the briefcase she had left propped against a wall. Though she knew perfectly well that she had been hired to decorate the house to enhance the sale value of all the houses in the subdivision, she felt no compunction whatever in utilizing artistic license in executing the ideas stimulating her imagination.

In Laura's mind, the house and the man were one. She would decorate the house as if it were Hank's home.

She was bent over the work island in the center of the large kitchen, jotting down ideas, when Hank found her hours later. As had happened earlier in her office, Laura didn't hear him approach.

"Getting anywhere?"

Startled by the low attractive sound of his voice, she dropped her pen and turned around. "Don't do that!"

"What?" The crinkles at the corners of his eyes betrayed Hank's amusement.

Laura made an impatient sound. "You know what. Don't creep up on me like that."

"Me? Creep?" Hank managed to look injured and innocent at the same time. "I never creep. It's against my religion."

Her lips trembled with suppressed laughter. "What religion is that?" she asked sweetly. "The church of the reformed idiots?"

Hank raised a hand to level a long index finger at her. "Close," he said, grinning like a member in good standing in the congregation.

"Yeah. Right." Laura unconsciously echoed Megan's current favorite expression. Frowning, she glanced around. "Was there anything in particular you wanted?" Spotting her pen, she picked it up and looked at him. "Or is this your normal pest-break period?"

Hank laughed; Laura decided she liked the sound much too much. "I didn't stop by just to pester you. There really was something I wanted to ask you."

Thinking, *here it comes,* Laura smoothed away her frown and arched her eyebrows. "Yes?"

"Did you have lunch?"

Lunch? Her frown was back in place. Lunch! Anticipating a proposition, his mundane question threw her. "No." She shook her head, as if attempting to clear her thoughts—which she was. "Why?"

"Because I didn't, either, and it's nearly dinnertime," Hank answered. "And I'm hungry. Aren't you?"

Laura was slightly amazed by the realization of the hours that had slipped by. "Now that you mention it," she said on a soft burst of laughter, "I believe I am hungry."

Stepping to one side of the doorway, Hank made a deep bow from the waist. "In that case, Ms. Seaton, lunch is served in the living room."

"The living room?" Laura asked, envisioning the stark emptiness of the huge room.

"Yes, ma'am," Hank replied. He made a sweeping movement with his arm. "After you."

The living room was filled with warmth and light from the long windows facing west. Tiny dust motes shimmered on the air like minute gold coins. A canvas drop cloth had been spread in the center of the floor. On the cloth were two tall white bags with the name of a fast-food restaurant emblazoned diagonally in scarlet across the side.

Laura's taste buds were activated at the sight of the familiar name. "A picnic?" she exclaimed. Following the scent of baked potatoes, she sank to her knees and lowered her head to sniff delicately at one of the open bags.

"It was either this or stand at the counter to eat." Hank came to stand beside her. "I hope you like baked potatoes."

"Love 'em," Laura admitted, laughing up at him. "With cheddar cheese?" she asked hopefully.

"And butter and broccoli..." Crossing his ankles, Hank lowered himself to the floor. "And there are beef sandwiches with horseradish sauce, and tossed salads," he continued, plucking the items he mentioned from the bags and arranging them on the cloth. "Since I didn't know what dressing you prefer, I brought one of each." He drew a handful of small plastic packets from the bottom of a bag. "There's Italian, Russian, blue cheese and buttermilk ranch." He dropped the packets onto the cloth.

"Buttermilk ranch," Laura said, easing herself down onto the canvas. "What? No soft drinks?" Her hazel eyes were bright with a teasing gleam.

"Soft drinks! With a gourmet meal like this?" He made a face and reached into a bag to withdraw a ruby-red bottle with a long slender neck. "Cabernet...California, of course."

"Oh, of course." Though Laura managed to keep her tone suitably solemn, her shoulders shook with suppressed laughter. "You did say we were having beef."

"Correct." Hank placed a foil-wrapped sandwich in front of her. Dipping into a bag, he retrieved the plastic containers of baked potatoes and salads, then handed her plastic utensils wrapped in a paper napkin. "Since I'm out of stemmed glasses," he murmured, easing the cork from the bottle, "we'll have to drink the wine from Styrofoam cups."

"Well, it is a picnic, after all." Laura indicated the food with an airy wave of her hand. "At least there are no creepy-crawly things to contend with."

"Excellent point." Hank grinned. "Dig in."

Laura did, savoring every morsel of the indoor picnic à la fast food. The wine was full-bodied, the potato was steamy and scrumptious, the salad was crisp and the beef had never before tasted quite so tender.

Hank ate two sandwiches to her one, and even polished off the half of potato she couldn't finish.

The conversation consisted of the occasional murmured remark while they ate. But after his food had disappeared, Hank asked the one question guaranteed to loosen Laura's tongue. "So," he said, glancing around at the empty room. "Have you come up with any ideas for decorating this barn?"

"Barn!" Laura cried. "Hank, this is a beautiful house! And it's going to be a pleasure to decorate it."

Hank's very masculine lips curved into a very satisfied smile. "Glad you like it." Tossing his napkin aside, he stretched out on the floor and propped his head on one hand. "I designed it." He tossed the information out as carelessly as he'd discarded his napkin.

Laura's smile curved softly with approval. "I thought as much." She swept the area with an appreciative glance. "It reflects you."

Hank managed to frown and grin at the same time. "Thank you . . . I think." His gaze followed the path of hers. "In what way does it reflect me?"

Laura raised her eyebrows. "You want me to enumerate?"

"I insist."

"It reflects you in every way." Laura flicked her hand in an encompassing arc. "It's big. It has strong clean lines. It looks warm and inviting while retaining a hint of cool austerity." She faced his widening grin with a calm expression. "It's solid, dependable, a structure one can trust."

Hank went still. His indolently stretched out body grew taut with tension. His grin faded. His relaxed features tightened with intent. "You believe I'm trustworthy?" His amber eyes bored into the depths of hers.

"Intuitively," Laura replied at once. She gave him a probing look. "Aren't you?"

A long moment of silence drew out the sudden tension crackling in the space between them. Then Hank laughed, and the tension scattered like swirling dust motes on the warm air. "Yes, as a matter of fact, I am." His voice was low, attractive, sexy. "Does being trustworthy mean I can't carry out my plans for the two of us?"

All the tension gathered again, inside Laura. Her nerves hummed with it, her spine tingled with it, her erratic breathing betrayed it. "Plans?" Her throat became parched. "What plans?"

Hank's smile was slow, exciting, unnerving. He cocked an eyebrow and raised his arm in a smooth, deceptively lazy motion. She stiffened when his warm fingers brushed the curve of her throat. "Don't panic. I won't hurt you," he murmured as his fingertips tested the tautness beneath her silky skin. "Didn't you just say you trusted me intuitively?"

"Yes...but... What are you doing?" Laura's voice dwindled to a rough whisper as his hand slid around her nape. "Hank?" Her breath caught on his name as she felt herself being drawn toward him by the gently applied pressure of his fingers.

"I'm going to kiss you." Hank's voice had dropped to a caressing murmur.

Laura was close enough to feel the heat from his body. The scent of wine on his breath was more intoxicating to her senses than the cabernet she'd drunk with the meal. The sensation was too pleasurable. Laura forced herself to protest. "Wh-what if I don't want you to kiss me?"

Hank's amber eyes glittered with amusement. "In that case," he murmured, applying the slight pressure of his hand to bring her lips to within a breath of his, "I'm afraid I will have to insist."

He insists a lot, was the last coherent thought to form in Laura's mind.

Hank's lips tested hers, tentatively, teasingly, and then he molded his mouth to hers. Sensations zigzagged through Laura's body, colliding in a burst of sheer joy. The world fell away, the room dissolved. Time and place became abstract ideas. The here and the now became paramount. The here of Hank's mouth, taking pleasure, giving it back. The now of

Hank's embrace, drawing her down to the comfort of a drop cloth on a bare wood floor and beneath the crushing luxury of his hard body.

The hungry penetration of his tongue into her mouth unleashed passion deeply suppressed inside Laura. Raw desire ran rampant through her trembling body, the fire of need in response to the devastating effects of Hank's expertise.

Helpless before the onslaught, Laura lost her carefully cultivated concepts of propriety and self-preservation. Mindlessly obeying urgent commands from within, she circled Hank's waist with her arms and allowed her hands the delicious freedom of exploring the curve of his spine and the tightly laced muscles of his broad back. Parting her lips, she gave her mouth free rein, returning his kisses with a greed born of years of repressed hunger.

Hank's straining body pressed hers to the hard floor. Laura didn't mind; she didn't even feel the unresisting wood against her back. While her mouth remained fused to his, while her tongue engaged in an erotic duel with his, all other considerations were reduced to ash in the conflagration of pleasure given and received.

It was at once exhilarating and exhausting, and it was not nearly enough. Hank's hand sought and found the soft fullness of her breast. A low growl of approval vibrated deep in his throat when he discovered the hard readiness of the aching crest. Impatience directed the hand he thrust between them to begin a quest for the button of her blouse. The touch of his fingertips on her bare skin activated an alarm at the edge of Laura's consciousness. She tore her mouth from his in reaction to the silent warning.

"No!"

Hank reared back to stare at her with sheer disbelief. "No?" he repeated in a shell-shocked tone. His breathing was ragged, his features were strained, his eyes were clouded by the passion searing his mind and body. "Laura..." His voice was swallowed by a groan.

"Hank, I...can't." Feeling the same crushing sense of deprivation mirrored in his face, Laura gasped for breath before continuing. "I want to...but I can't."

Placing his palms on the floor on either side of her shoulders, Hank levered his torso up, putting a distance between them. He stared into her wide pleading eyes and inhaled deep harsh-sounding breaths. "You want to?"

Laura was nearly undone by the note of longing coiled through his uneven voice. Amazed by the effort required to lift her arm, she stroked her fingers along his clenched jaw. "The response of my body betrays me," she murmured, thrilling to his tremor of response to her feather-light caress. "How can I deny it?" Unable to resist an inner desire, she stroked one finger over his compressed mouth. A gasp caught painfully in her throat when his lips parted to capture her finger. Heat flared anew deep inside her as Hank slowly drew her finger inside his mouth, sucking gently as he bathed the tip with his tongue.

"Hank..." Every sensation and confusing emotion Laura was feeling was contained within the whisper of his name.

"I know," he murmured as she drew her hand to safety. His features taut, he dragged in a deep breath and then pushed his body away and to the side of hers on the floor. "Lord, Laura, I want you so much I can't think straight." He turned his head to gaze into the hazel allure of her eyes. "Nothing like this has ever happened to me before."

A fluid expression brightened Laura's eyes; a melting smile curved her soft mouth. "Or to me," she confessed. "I want you to know that I haven't been playing any kind of teasing games with you." Her voice was unsteady with concern.

Hank gave her a chiding look. "I know that." His lips twisted in a wry smile. "Hell, I doubt there's any man who recognizes the signs better than I do."

His arm was touching hers from shoulder to wrist, and Laura could feel the tension that suddenly tightened his muscles and tendons. She hesitated an instant, then in a gesture of reassurance, slid her palm over the back of his hand. "You...ah, you've had experience with that type of teasing female?" she asked.

His brief burst of laughter was devoid of humor. "I was all set to marry one." His lips slanted bitterly. "My best friend rescued me from certain disaster a week before the wedding."

The hard sound of his voice made Laura uneasy, and yet she couldn't contain the question that sprang to her tongue. "Did your friend talk you out of marrying her?"

Hank slowly moved his head back and forth on the floor. "Oh, no. He went far beyond talk—and me," he said dryly, growing still to stare into her eyes again. "My friend and supposed-to-be best man eloped with her himself."

"Oh, Hank." Laura didn't know why she felt the pain he must have suffered, she only knew she did. "I'm sorry."

Turning his hand, he entwined their fingers. "Don't be. The jerk did me a favor." He smiled a slow sexy smile. "If he hadn't run off to California with her, I probably wouldn't be here today, either in this business or on this floor, now, with you."

Laura felt complimented and confused. "Why not this business?"

His shoulders rippled in a shrug. "Because she was determined to talk me into selling out and relocating in California."

"And you'd have given in to her?"

He smiled derisively. "Odds are that I would have, eventually. You see, I had bought her little-girl-lost act and had convinced myself that I was in love with her."

Laura was quiet for several moments, worrying a nagging question. Then she blurted it out, if softly. "How can you be positive I wasn't putting on an act a few minutes ago?"

Hank laughed and squeezed her hand. "I'm positive," he said. "You weren't acting, and I know it."

"But how do you know?" she persisted.

"Your eyes."

Laura blinked. "My eyes?"

"Umm," he murmured, nodding his strong chin. "Laura, don't you know that your eyes mirror every one of your emotions?"

Her eyes flew wide. "They do?"

"Yes, they do." His smile tilted into a teasing taunt. "Do you want to know what I see mirrored in those beautiful hazel depths right now?"

Laura's lashes swept down, but curiosity prevailed and she immediately looked up at him again. "What do you see?"

"I see confusion caused by the intensity of passion recently experienced, and a hint of shock at finding yourself lying on the floor beside a man you barely know."

Laura gaped at him; he had described her feelings exactly. "I had no idea I was so transparent!" she exclaimed, chagrined at the very notion of being so easy to read.

"Not transparent, honest," Hank corrected her. "You can't possibly know what a delight it is for me to gaze into the eyes of a genuinely honest woman."

Laura forgot her chagrin to take exception to the derogatory remark. "Hank Branson, there are a lot of honest women in the world!"

"Oh, yeah?" Hank retorted with a grin. "Name two."

Not for an instant giving thought to the ludicrousness of their argument—considering their prone positions—Laura bristled and replied, "My assistant, Ginnie, for one, and my daughters..." Her voice deserted her. Her daughters...Megan!

"What is it? What's wrong?"

"Megan." Laura's voice was subdued.

"Megan?" He frowned. "What about her?"

"She thinks she's in love with you."

"What!" Hank jackknifed into a sitting position, unconsciously and unceremoniously pulling her up also with a tug of their laced fingers. "What are you talking about?" He stared at her in blank confusion.

Laura required a few seconds to regain her equilibrium; along with it she gained a feeling of relief from his obvious ignorance of Megan's feelings for him. He caught her attention by releasing her hand to grasp her shoulders.

"Laura, answer me." Hank's voice held a definite command. "Where did you ever get the idea that Megan 'thinks' she's in love with me?"

"She told me."

His expression went blank again. "When?"

She exhaled in a tired-sounding sigh. "The other night, when we were cleaning up after the party."

His fingers flexed into the tender flesh of her upper arms. "You were discussing me?"

"No!" Laura bit her lips, then lifted her shoulders in a helpless shrug. "Not really," she qualified. "Megan and Brooke were discussing the party. Your name came up during the conversation." She glanced down, afraid he'd read her evasion in her eyes.

"My name came up in the course of conversation, and Megan just happened to mention the fact that she thinks she's in love with me?" His voice held blatant disbelief.

Laura swallowed; her voice cracked anyway. "Basically, yes."

His fingers flexed again. She winced. He eased his grip at once. "I'm sorry." His voice was tight and strained. "Laura, I hope to God you haven't been thinking that I encouraged Megan in any way."

"I..." She glanced up, and all the uncertainty she'd felt was mirrored in her eyes.

When he spoke, his voice was intense. "Laura, I swear by my life that I have never even thought about

Megan in any way other than a lovely pleasant young girl.'' He removed one hand from her arm to rake it through his hair, ruffling the already shaggy strands. ''Good grief!'' he exploded. ''I am nearly old enough to be her father! I never thought . . . dreamed—'' He broke off to look at her with desperation. ''Laura, I swear—''

Laura interrupted him in a tone of utter conviction. ''I believe you, Hank.'' But, though the uncertainty had been removed, she knew she still had a problem, and it was growing bigger with her deepening attraction to him.

''There are no lingering doubts in your mind?'' Hank studied her intently.

''None.''

He exhaled on a sharp sound of relief. Then he frowned and sprang to his feet. ''Dammit! What are we going to do?''

''About what?'' Craning her neck, Laura looked up at him in confusion. ''Megan?''

''Of course, Megan!'' he exclaimed, thrusting out his hand impatiently to help her to stand.

Catching sight of her wrinkled skirt, Laura frowned and began smoothing her hands over the material. ''There's nothing we can do, Hank. More than being in love, I believe Megan is in a state of infatuation due to proximity to an attractive man she admires.'' She started when his fingers grasped her chin to raise her head. She smiled into his scowl. ''She's young. She'll get over it, Hank.''

''I know that.'' As if he couldn't resist, his fingers deserted her chin for her mouth. ''What I meant was . . .'' His eyes lowered to observe the play of his stroking fingers. His voice deepened. "What are we going to do about seeing each other?"

A combined thrill of anticipation and trepidation shot through Laura. She wanted to see him, be with him. At the same time, she was fearful about being alone with him again, not because she didn't trust Hank, but because she no longer trusted herself. And yet, since she couldn't deny herself the pleasure of hearing him say it, she asked the question burning in her mind and body. "You want to see me...on a nonprofessional basis?"

"Laura, please, don't start playing games now." He lowered his mouth to give her a kiss that was too brief in duration and unsatisfactory in content. "I don't wish to hurt Megan in any way, but I want to see you...on any basis." He brushed his lips tantalizingly over hers. She felt him smile at her indrawn breath. "Since I obviously can't come to your home, will you come to my apartment tomorrow evening?"

Laura gasped again, but for a different reason. She had never before in her life visited a man at his apartment. "I..." She wanted to say yes, but it was too soon, much too soon. "I can't," she finally answered.

Hank lifted his head to frown at her. "Then where? Will you meet me at a restaurant for dinner?"

Will I be expected to pay for the meal in bed later?

Laura dismissed the question at once; it no longer applied. Still, she made a bid for time to think. "I will need to come back here to the house tomorrow. Can I give you my answer then?"

Hank looked about to argue, but changed his mind. "Do I have a choice?" he asked wryly.

Laura smiled. "No."

His shrug betrayed impatience. "Then I guess I'll have to wait till then."

Struck by a sudden desire to grant him anything, everything he might want of her, Laura clung to her senses and glanced at her watch. "I must go!" she exclaimed, turning away to retrieve her purse and briefcase from the kitchen.

Hank was waiting for her at the front door. "You forgot something," he said. Reaching out, he fastened the buttons he'd managed to open before she'd stopped him.

The brush of his fingers on the material covering her breasts sent new sensations of excitement tingling through Laura. Against her will, she lowered her gaze to his hands.

"You forgot something else." The rough velvet sound of his voice drew her eyes to his. "You forgot to kiss me goodbye."

"Hank, I must..." Her voice was lost inside his mouth.

With a murmured groan, Hank gathered her close, shocking her, thrilling her with the hard strength of his body. For long delicious moments, Laura clung to his mouth and his strength, then she pulled away, blindly reaching for the door.

"I must go," she said, avoiding the temptation of him by stepping outside. "It's late." Turning away, she ran for the safety of her car.

Five

It's later than you think.

Hank laughed softly at the thought. Standing in the open doorway of the model house, he squinted against the glare of late afternoon sunlight and watched the plume of dust that had been raised by Laura's car.

Laura. The thrill he felt from just thinking her name dried the laughter in Hank's throat. Turning abruptly, he strode into the house and straight to the drop cloth in the center of the living room. A tremor crept the length of his spine as he stared at the rumpled cloth he had taken such care to smooth out on the hardwood floor. Together he and Laura had rumpled that cloth.

Together.

Memories flooded Hank's mind and washed through his body, reigniting the fire of passion in his blood. His fingers grew warm in remembrance of the too brief thrill derived from touching her silky flesh. His mouth grew dry with the memory of being caressed by hers. His muscles bunched, his body ached ... for Laura, Laura.

Hearing the harsh sound of his shallow breaths, Hank tore his gaze from the cloth and glanced around the spacious room. Even though she was gone, he could feel her presence surrounding him. Impossible as it seemed, Laura's essence was manifest in the room as if, within the few hours of her occupancy, she had claimed the place as her own, leaving a part of herself within its walls.

Hank's nostrils twitched then flared, and he inhaled deeply to capture the hint of her scent lingering on the still air. The exciting woman scent of her pierced his heart in its direct descent to the most masculine part of him.

It's later than you think!

This time the same thought took on altogether different and far-reaching connotations. He had just met her, barely knew her, but Hank had the odd feeling that he had known Laura all his life and yet had been waiting, waiting for her, only her.

The feeling was more than a little weird. Never having experienced anything quite like it before, Hank wasn't sure exactly how to deal with the sensation. Narrowing his eyes, he looked around once more, absorbing the elusive scent of her into his body, his senses, his emotions. She was gone, and yet he could see her, feel her, taste her. An anticipatory quiver in his taut muscles brought Hank to his senses.

Shrugging himself out of bemusement, he bent and scooped the cloth from the floor. Turning, he strode from the room. He had neglected his work long enough; he didn't have time to stand around fantasying over a woman. Still, Hank paused at the door to glance over his shoulder into the living room.

Laura had said the place was a reflection of him, but now it seemed to reflect her, as well.

Spooky.

Shaking his head with sharp impatience, Hank pulled open the door. Either he was crazy or he was already more involved than he had ever planned on becoming. Slamming the door behind him, he headed for the dusty van.

"Take it slow, Branson," he advised himself in a mutter. "You could damn well be in for a very big fall."

Despite the muttered warning, Hank intuitively knew that he would never sell the model house. His mind rebelled at the very thought of strangers living, laughing and loving in the house he now thought of as his and Laura's special place.

The thought he'd had earlier sprang into his mind as Hank started the van.

It's later than you think.

But this time, instead of laughing, Hank cursed and told himself to get moving back to the real world. His palm smacked the gearshift, and the van shot forward.

Fortunately for Hank's peace of mind, if not the air that turned blue around him, he walked into a problem when he entered the house presently under construction. His men were trying to work around a mess created by the subcontracted plumbing crew. He was hit by their loud complaints the instant he stepped from the van. The anger that seared through him on sight of the mess burned away all the contemplation and confusion in his mind. His language colorful enough to educate a seasoned marine, Hank strode into the building and set about restoring order. Darkness had long since fallen before he was free to leave the site.

Hank pulled off his work boots inside the door of his sparsely furnished apartment. He began removing his dusty clothes as he crossed the living room, heading for his bedroom. He wanted a long hot bath, a thick rare steak and eight solid hours of sleep...in that order.

He had wallowed in the shower and was three-quarters through the steak when the phone rang. He considered answering it himself then, shrugging, decided to let the answering machine pick it up. He was slicing into the steak when he heard the tone and then the sound of his brother's voice. The fork bearing a piece of beef hovered midway between his mouth and the plate as Hank listened to the message.

"It's Luke, Hank. I'm coming home...to stay, and was hoping you could put me up until I can find a place. I'll be there Saturday. Talk to you then."

Yep, that was Luke, all right, short and to the point, Hank mused, absently chewing the rapidly cooling meat. Deciding he needed a beer, he carried his plate to the sink and rinsed it and stashed it in the dishwasher before pulling open the refrigerator. Popping the top of an icy can, he took three deep swallows of the cold brew while mulling over the ramifications of his brother's call.

After eight years, Luke was coming home...for good. Great, Hank thought, sighing. Luke was just what he needed at this particular point in his life—and in his 'almost' relationship with Laura. Luke and his bitterness and cynicism.

It wasn't that Hank didn't love his younger brother; he did. He not only loved Luke, he admired him. In Hank's personal and professional opinion, Luke was one of the finest architects in the country, if not the world. He had been a tremendous help, practically and inspirationally, to Hank while he was setting up his company during his own period of bitterness. And, as Hank hadn't seen his brother in more than five years, it would be wonderful to see him, or at least it should be wonderful...but...

But he was near the point of distraction about a woman. Hank exhaled. And Luke was bitter about women.

Great.

He took another swallow of beer, grimaced, then set the can in the sink. He didn't really want the brew. He didn't really want any further agitation, either. But...Hank shrugged. Luke was coming, and that was that. He'd deal with it on Saturday. In the meantime, he needed some sleep. Laura would be at the house sometime tomorrow.

Raising his arms above his head, Hank yawned and stretched luxuriously. *Tomorrow.* Anticipation coiled inside his midsection. Savoring the sense of pending excitement, Hank strolled from the kitchen to his bedroom. He hit the bed like a lead weight. Sheer weariness tugged his eyelids down. After another sigh, his breathing became deeper. A final thought carried Hank into slumber.

Saturday could take care of itself. Laura would be at the house tomorrow.

"I was just about ready to phone the police and request they send out a search party for you." Ginnie's grin belied her statement, but her eyes betrayed genuine concern. "I was beginning to fear the man had actually done you bodily injury."

He did me bodily something! Laura reflected, smiling to conceal her inner reaction to the thought. "Well, as you can see for yourself," she said, "I am perfectly fine."

"Umm," Ginnie responded noncommittally. "So, how did it go?" She raised her eyebrows.

Grateful for the safer topic, Laura launched into an enthusiastic report. "The house is terrific! I'm going to love decorating it."

Ginnie's expression grew pensive. "And the man?" she said softly. "Is he terrific, also?"

The man!

Laura shivered.

Ginnie noticed. A wry smile curved her lips. "Your Mr. Hank Branson is rather delicious looking," she observed.

Laura visibly jolted. "He isn't *my* Hank Branson!"

"Yet," Ginnie murmured. "But, from his insistence on seeing you personally today, I'd make a guess that he easily could be."

"No!" Laura shook her head to emphasize her rejection of Ginnie's observation. "Hank isn't looking for a serious involvement."

"Who is?" Ginnie retorted. "Are you?"

Laura's color fluctuated from pale to pink. "No." Her voice was faint, her tone strained. "You know I'm not."

Ginnie smiled with compassionate amusement. "The problem is, involvement sometimes finds us, whether or not we happen to be looking for it."

"I suppose." Laura's tone lacked conviction. "But, my problem is, it's never found me before."

Ginnie laughed and pushed her chair away from the desk. "No kidding?" she drawled, picking up her briefcase and shoulder bag. "You weren't involved with your husband?"

"Yes, of course!" Laura looked startled. "But that wasn't the same... Oh, you know what I mean."

"Sure, I know what you mean." Ginnie slipped into her suit jacket as she walked to the door. "But, between us girls, I think an involvement would be the best thing for you."

"Why?" Laura exclaimed.

Without pausing, Ginnie said over her shoulder, "Because I think it's long past time someone rattled your comfortable little cage."

For an instant, Laura was too surprised to respond. Then it was too late. Ginnie set the tiny bells jangling as she shut the showroom door behind her.

Laura mulled over Ginnie's parting shot as she locked the shop and then drove home. Was she living in a comfortable cage? Her immediate reaction was to reject the consideration as utterly ridiculous. Her life and life-style were of her own choosing and making. She was comfortable, yes, in a personal and material way. Her children were healthy and happy. Her business was thriving. And, if not in the least rich, she was solvent, with a respectable bank balance and a modest investment portfolio.

So, yes, she was comfortable, Laura thought, smiling complacently as she drove into the driveway bordering the small neat backyard of the town house. She had everything any woman could possibly ask for, and she couldn't imagine why Ginnie had made that remark about a cage or why she should feel Laura needed rattling.

But what about her inner emotional life?

The question sprang with shocking clarity into Laura's mind, straight out of the depths of the passion she'd experienced that afternoon.

A thrill quivered through her, leaving a wake of longing so intense Laura felt unable to move for several minutes. Within the double cocoon of car and garage, removed from the intrusive noises of the outside world, Laura sat trembling, listening to the silent messages being sent to her from her responsively shivering body.

She wanted, wanted . . .

Drawing a sharp breath, Laura tried to block the messages, garble the signals. She had always been able to control her emotions. Even as a young woman, her mind had dictated her response and reaction to her husband, and she had loved him with all her heart.

But, this time, her control slipped from her grasp. Her emotions broke through, inflaming her senses. She had spent too many years without experiencing the reassuring embrace of strong arms, the stroking caress of masculine hands, the ardor of a hungry mouth and the stirring pressure of a taut male form straining against her pliant body.

She wanted Hank Branson.

The ache in Laura's fingers snapped her out of introspection, back to reality. For a moment she stared in mute wonder at her hands gripping the steering wheel, then sighed as she consciously loosened her hold.

What was she going to do?

Laura pondered the question as she pushed her door open and stepped from the car. Her earlier decision to avoid Hank was no longer viable. Not only had she accepted the commission to decorate his model house, she had literally rolled around on the floor with him! She had returned his kisses, his caresses, his passion . . . and had yearned for much more. In truth, she still ached with the yearning for full possession by him!

Embarrassment heated Laura's skin from the base of her throat to her cheekbones. Her hand paused in the act of turning the knob on the garage door leading into the kitchen of the town house. She drew in deep breaths in an attempt to regulate the erratic beat of her heart. She had to appear calm. It was late. In all probability Megan would be home. Straightening her spine, Laura opened the door and walked into the kitchen.

Megan was standing at the sink, tearing lettuce for a salad. The smile she flashed at the sight of her mother sent a sharp shaft of pain through Laura's chest.

"Hi, Mom, you're late." Megan deposited the last of the lettuce into the wooden salad bowl, then turned to pour a cup of coffee for Laura.

"Mmm, thanks," Laura murmured, setting her purse and briefcase aside before taking the cup from Megan. "Where's Ruth?" she asked, appreciatively sniffing the scent of roasting chicken permeating the room.

"Laundry room." Megan's smile widened. "She offered to iron a blouse for me if I'd fix the salad." Gazing intently at Laura, her smile gave way to a tiny frown. "You look beat," she observed. "Rough day?"

A series of scenes flashed through Laura's mind: Ginnie, looking fresh and delectable as she left the showroom to meet with Hank; Hank, looking dusty and determined when he came to the showroom to collect her; the model house, looking exactly like the home Laura had always dreamed of owning and, the most vivid of all, the memory of their impromptu picnic on the living room floor.

Rough day? Laura stifled a groan and, from somewhere, produced a pale imitation of a smile. "Not rough," she finally answered, "but rather exciting."

"Oh?" Megan looked interested. "In what way?"

Laura stalled for time by sipping the steaming coffee. It was Wednesday. Megan worked in Hank's office on Thursday and Friday afternoons and all day Saturday. Laura knew she had to tell her daughter about her agreement to decorate the model house, because if she didn't, Megan would find out in the office and naturally wonder why her mother hadn't mentioned it. Laura hesitated briefly, then took the plunge into explanation.

"I acquired an account today that could possibly broaden my business considerably."

"That's great!" Megan exclaimed. "But I didn't think your business needed broadening."

"Every business needs broadening," Laura said wryly, carefully placing the hot cup on the table before removing her suit jacket.

Megan shrugged. "Whatever you say. So, what account did you manage to snare?"

Laura moistened her lips. "Branson Construction," she answered distinctly.

"Branson Construction?" Megan frowned. "Why would Hank hire an interior decorator?"

Laura's frown mirrored her daughter's. Didn't Megan know why Hank would hire a decorator? Megan had been working for Hank for eight months. Hadn't he had other model homes decorated during that time period? "For the model house at the new subdivision," she replied. "Why else?"

"Beats me." Megan shrugged. "As far as I know, Hank has never bothered to have a model unit furnished."

The information sent a thrill dancing along Laura's spine. Had Hank really wanted a decorator or . . .

"Oh, hi, Laura, I didn't know you were home." Ruth bustled into the room carrying a jungle-print blouse on a padded hanger. "Did Megan get you coffee?"

"Hi, and yes, she did." Laura indicated the cup with a flick of one hand and wryly mused on how predictable she was, down to needing a cup of coffee the minute she got home from work. "Dinner smells delicious."

"And it's almost ready," Ruth said. "You have just enough time to have a shower and change, if you want to."

Grateful for the opportunity to escape further questioning by Megan, Laura picked up her cup and headed for the doorway. "I do want to. I'll be back in fifteen minutes."

While the warm pulsating shower spray sluiced over her tired body, soothing the tension within, Laura pondered on the importance of the information Megan had innocently imparted to her about Hank, and his possible motives.

To Megan's knowledge, Hank had never before hired a professional decorator for a model house or had as much as bothered to furnish one of the homes. Yet he had commissioned Laura for that purpose.

Hmm. Her expression contemplative, Laura stepped from the shower and absently dried off. Repressing the quiver her contemplation produced, she tossed the damp towel into the white wicker hamper in a corner, twisted the cap off a bottle of scented lotion, then methodically smoothed the creamy liquid into her soft skin.

Had Hank seriously wanted a decorator to furnish the model house to enhance its sale value, or had he simply wanted . . .

Laura's trembling fingers halted midstroke on her slender calf. Moving slowly, she lowered her narrow foot from the rim of the tub and turned to examine her nude reflection in the full-length mirror on the bathroom door.

Was this what Hank wanted? she asked herself, studying the image reflected back at her. In Laura's biased opinion, the image wasn't anything to get excited about.

The woman in the mirror was, first and foremost, to her way of thinking, within shouting distance of her fortieth birthday. In addition, Laura felt certain she was depressingly average looking. Frowning, she took stock of the average-looking woman taking stock of her.

There was definitely nothing unique about her height of five feet six inches. Her figure was okay, Laura supposed, but a trifle slim, if gently rounded. She had always despaired of her breasts because of their lack of size, even though they were well formed and surprisingly still firm, taut and up-tilted. For her height and weight, her waist was all right, being neither too tiny nor too thick. Her hipline was passable, she mused, homing in on the smooth curve from her waist to the top of her legs. A sigh whispered through her lips as she gazed at the barely discernible mound of her belly, which no amount of exercise had flattened since Megan's advent. She deliberately skimmed over the small pale stretch marks, which gave visual proof that she had carried two infants to full term.

Not at all enthralled with her self-examination, Laura was tempted to turn away from the image she habitually avoided, but determination kept her rooted to the floor, determination to ascertain exactly what it was about her that had sparked Hank's interest.

In all honesty Laura had to admit that her legs were not at all bad. And, in truth, she had slim attractive feet. Wonderful, she thought, trailing her critical gaze up the long slender length of her legs from slim ankles to smooth thighs. Continuing her perusal, Laura noted the flatness of her midsection, hurried by her B-cup breasts, then settled her brooding eyes on her mirrored visage.

Again, as far as Laura was concerned, her reflection revealed nothing above average; her features were good but not spectacular. Her eyes were a clear hazel. As a girl and young woman, Laura wished they were a deep mysterious green. And what, she mused, could anyone say about her hair, other than that it was brown? Oh, her hair was thick, and silky to the touch, but it was brown—not auburn, not chestnut, not even ash, but plain average brown.

But her skin was good. Laura brightened as she narrowed her eyes on her face. In actual fact, her complexion was more than good, it was exceptional, and Laura knew it. She diligently cared for her unlined translucent skin, which afforded her the appearance of a younger woman. And her eyelashes were long, with a natural upward curve requiring no assistance from an eyelash curler.

Big deal.

With that final assessment, Laura turned away from the mirror, her conviction of looking rather average unaltered. In her estimation, she was decidedly not a raving beauty like, for instance, Ginnie Devlon. And yet, Hank had passed up the opportunity to become acquainted with Ginnie in favor of being with her.

Why? Laura worried the question like a sore tooth while she dressed in casual slacks and a soft cotton shirt. Why, when he obviously appealed to women of all ages, and very likely had his pick of any one of them, had Hank Branson, handsome, thirty-six and extremely eligible, singled out Laura Seaton, widow, mother of two and uncomfortably close to forty years of age?

Hank had very simply explained his reason for contacting her by claiming he was interested in a decorator, and as Megan worked for him, had naturally thought of her first. But, by his actions that afternoon, Hank seemed more interested in her personally than professionally.

And Megan maintained that he had never before furnished a model home, Laura reflected. Excitement coiled deep inside her at the memory of his frustration that afternoon when she'd said he'd have to wait for her answer. Was it possible Hank had used the house as an excuse, a ploy to make contact with her? she wondered. Did he in fact want the house decorated? Or did Hank want—

"Mother. Ruth's putting dinner on the table." Megan's call interrupted Laura's thoughts.

Squelching the quivering excitement playing havoc with her senses and sense, Laura called "Coming," and fastened a clip to anchor the twist she didn't recall pleating her hair into at the back of her head. Swinging away from her dressing table, she walked briskly from the room.

Speculation was getting her nowhere, Laura decided. As she descended the stairs, she recalled her last conversation with Hank. Before she'd reached the kitchen, she decided to tell Ruth not to expect her for dinner tomorrow night. She had told Hank she'd see him at the house tomorrow afternoon, and she wanted to spend time with him. And, if she had any sense at all, she concluded, she'd ask Hank point-blank to explain exactly why he had contacted her.

The prospect of confronting Hank about his intentions kept Laura in a state of anticipation through the rest of the evening and into the next day. She had to force down her meager breakfast of a small glass of grapefruit juice and a piece of wheat toast. She had to concentrate to deal coherently with several customers, both on the phone and in the showroom. She had to be on guard against a consistent urge to glance at her watch. And she had to endure the speculative looks Ginnie sent her way at regular intervals.

It was going on three when Laura told Ginnie she was leaving to keep an appointment and that she wouldn't be back that afternoon. As she walked from the showroom, she looked as cool and composed as usual; inside though, Laura felt like a basket case.

The model house was located on the outskirts of the subdivision. As she drove up to the house, Laura envisioned it set like a jewel into the center of immaculately landscaped grounds. Unlike the many other subdivisions she had seen, the houses were distanced from one another on spacious individual lots.

After stepping from the car, Laura ran a slow thoughtful gaze over the area and silently applauded Hank's keen symmetrical sense and astute planning. Smiling faintly, she concluded that Hank would probably find himself besieged by eager buyers for the unique properties when construction and the landscaping were completed, if not before then.

Laura's smile faded as she approached the unusual front door, which was attractively painted Williamsburg blue. What if the door was locked? Hank hadn't

thought to give her a key. Reaching out, she grasped
the old-fashioned latch-style door handle. She pressed
down her thumb and pushed. The door swung open.

It was like coming home. The thought struck Laura
the instant she crossed the threshold. Her heels rang
with a familiar-sounding click on the flagstone floor
of the foyer. The click ceased abruptly at the entranceway to the living room.

Her breath constricting in her chest, Laura stared at
the hardwood flooring in the center of the living room.
With her mind's eye she saw two figures entwined on
a bed of canvas, immune to the hardness of the floor
beneath them and unconcerned with the nearby debris of an impromptu picnic.

Feeling again the heat of Hank's mouth on hers, the
strength of his body straining against the softness of
her own, Laura's fingers dug into the briefcase she was
clutching. She had thought to continue jotting down
ideas for the living room. On second thought, she'd
begin with the bedrooms—they didn't hold any memories for her. Spinning around, she ran for the stairs.

Laura immediately lost all sense of time. She had no
idea if Hank wanted only one bedroom or all of them
furnished but, once she'd started, there was no stop-
ping her. Ideas tumbled into her mind faster than she
could jot them down. She could "see" exactly how
every bedroom, each bathroom, should look. She
saved the master bedroom for last . . . not unlike des-
sert at the end of a sumptuous meal.

In reality, the bedroom was a master suite, com-
prised of an enormous sleeping room, a spacious
dressing room and a large bathroom that was ap-
pointed with everything imaginable. Laura wryly

mused that a family of three could set up housekeeping in the suite quite comfortably.

Although she tried to conjure up ideas for appealing yet impersonal furnishings for the bedroom, Laura's rebellious mind persisted in presenting designs reflecting the personality of one particular man. To her mind, the room belonged to Hank Branson. Her inner eye could see no one other than Hank in residence. Standing in the middle of the bedroom, eyes closed, Laura could see Hank relaxing in the hot tub, choosing attire in the dressing room, sprawled on a—

"It cries out for a king-size bed."

Laura gasped aloud as her eyes flew open. Hank was lounging in the doorway, his shoulder resting against the frame in a pose similar to the one he'd struck the day before in her office. But today there was a decided difference in his appearance. Instead of the dusty work clothes and boots, he was wearing dark brown slacks, a tan sport coat, a pale blue silk shirt and gleaming wing-tip shoes.

Laura said the first thought that popped into her head. "You're dressed!"

A slow smile tugged at his mouth; Laura felt it to the soles of her feet. "You'd prefer it if I weren't?" Hank inquired in a suspiciously bland tone.

"No! Yes! I mean...!" Flustered, Laura wasn't sure what she meant. "Oh, you know what I mean!"

"Hmm." Hank nodded sagely. "You mean, I look clean and presentable this evening."

"This evening?" Frowning, Laura turned to glance through the window. The horizon was ablaze with pink and purple streaks left by the setting sun. "What time is it?"

Hank made a show of looking at his watch. "Exactly 6:49," he reported. "Time for a predinner drink."

"Drink?" Laura repeated, dry voiced.

"Hmm." Hank again nodded.

"Predinner?"

"Hmm."

"We're having dinner together?"

"You got it, honey."

Laura exhaled. She wanted to go with him, longed to go with him, but... "Hank, I explained about Megan."

"I know." A flash of annoyance flickered across his face. "No one will see us together where we're going."

Laura knew, but still she asked. "Where are we going?"

His slow smile returned to tantalize her. "To my place."

Six

Hank's apartment was something of a disappointment. Laura wasn't sure what she had expected, but she was certain the austere Spartan collection of rooms wasn't it. In a strange way, she was relieved. Her nerves had tautened with each successive mile between the subdivision and his building, which was located close to his business office near City Avenue in Philadelphia. And, had it not been for the fact that Hank had insisted they use his car and pick hers up later, Laura knew she would have turned around and dashed for the safety of her town house.

Fortunately for her peace of mind, her nervousness gave way to the designer in her on sight of the sparsely furnished apartment. A tiny frown drew her eyebrows together as she studied the living room. It simply was not Hank. It was wrong, all wrong. The few pieces of furniture in the apartment were altogether unsuitable for his rugged personality. The prints on the stark taupe walls were as cold and antiseptic looking as the chrome-and-leather furniture. And the curtains on the windows . . . Laura shuddered and turned away. She didn't even want to think about those blah wet-sand-colored curtains, never mind look at them!

"It's pretty depressing, isn't it?" Hank observed, sauntering into the room from the kitchen. He was holding a glass in each hand, fragile wine flutes that looked out of place in the too somber room.

With a murmured "Thank you," Laura accepted the glass he offered her. "It's certainly not you," she answered candidly, sweeping the room with a disdainful look.

Hank treated her to one of his soul-tingling smiles. "I'm glad to hear it," he drawled, grimacing as his gaze trailed hers. "I guess it's supposed to have mass appeal . . . or something."

Laura gave him a dry look as she tested the quality of the golden liquid in her glass. "Exquisite," she said, complimenting his taste. Then she laughed. "I refer to the wine, not your statement about the apartment."

"The hell with the apartment. I rented it furnished." Hank dismissed the place with a shrug. "You ought to do that more often."

"Do what?" Laura laughed again, a trifle breathlessly this time. Hank's eyes had taken on a molten amber glow.

"Laugh like that," he explained in a tone that matched the warmth of his eyes. "That soft husky laugh of yours does incredibly erotic things to my libido."

Flattered, flustered and suddenly extremely nervous again, Laura glanced away from the flaring heat in his eyes. "Hank..." She drew a quick breath and raised her eyes to his. "I don't quite know what to say."

Hank moved closer to her, a tender smile tilting his mouth. "You don't have to say anything." He tipped his glass at her. "To you," he toasted softly, "and me." He paused, then went on, "And to the house you'll be decorating for me."

Until the words were spoken aloud, Hank had never as much as considered keeping the model house for himself. But, the moment the words were spoken, he knew he'd never be able to bear seeing someone else in it. It was his house...and it was Laura's house. Shying away from the implications of the thought, Hank made an abrupt move toward the kitchen.

"I think I smell something about to burn," he explained when Laura threw him a puzzled look. "The bathroom's along that hallway," he motioned toward the passageway leading off of the living room. "You can freshen up while I serve dinner."

The look of relief that flickered over Laura's face both amused and hurt Hank. She was more than a little nervous of him, and he didn't like that. But she had agreed to come here with him, and that caused a warm sensation deep inside him.

The first time Hank singed a finger on the oven rack, he cursed fluently under his breath. The second time the metal seared his flesh, he grinned at himself. From all indications, it was abundantly clear that Laura wasn't the only nervous one in the apartment.

The realization was slightly amazing. It had been years since Hank had felt twinges of nervousness because of a woman. In fact, it had been the same number of years since his fiancée had eloped with his best friend. During the interval, Hank frankly hadn't cared enough about any one woman to feel nervous.

Now, he was sweating *and* nervous! Blaming the heat from the oven for the former, Hank slid the broiler tray from under the flame and onto the stove top, then quickly shut the oven door, closing in the heat. He burned his finger once more on the hot tray when he heard Laura enter the kitchen.

Damn fool! he thought, turning to grin crookedly at her. "I hope you like Delmonicos," he said, feeling his insides turn to mush at the apprehensive expression in her lovely hazel eyes. "I'm afraid my culinary skill is limited to broiled steak and a tossed salad." His legs went weak when she smiled at him.

"But you do open a mean bottle of wine," she murmured, extending her glass for a refill as she crossed the room to him. "And I love steak and salad." Her nostrils flared delicately as she sniffed. "Do I smell French bread?" she asked with endearing eagerness.

Bread? Hank mused, lost to everything but the delectable curve of her upper lip. *Bread? Holy....*

"Bread! Yes!" Grabbing the hot pad he'd tossed aside, Hank yanked the oven door open and pulled the long loaf from the rack. "I forgot it," he muttered, dropping the crusty bread into a long narrow basket.

"Can I help with anything?"

The feminine amusement woven through her tone should have rankled. Instead, Hank felt as if a weight had been lifted from his shoulders. If nothing else, his kitchen fumbling had produced one positive result—Laura's nervous tension had eased considerably. Suddenly starved—for more than mere food—Hank motioned to the refrigerator. "You can get the salad."

Laura dabbed at her mouth, set the napkin beside her plate and sat back in her chair, replete with food and mellowed with wine. "That was delicious," she said, smiling at Hank across the small table he'd placed near the living room windows.

Hank's return smile was wry. "It was steak and salad," he said disparagingly.

"But very good steak and salad," Laura persisted. "And don't forget the French bread."

"Perish the thought!" Hank laughed. "Would you like some coffee?"

Laura shook her head. "No, thank you. I haven't finished my wine." She held the flute up as proof.

Hank mirrored her action with the slender-necked bottle. "We still have this to finish."

Laura gave him an arch look. "Are you trying to get me tipsy?" She was teasing; she didn't feel in the least tipsy, simply mellow and relaxed.

Hank's reaction startled her. His expression turned grim, and with an abrupt movement, he reached across the table and plucked the glass from her fingers. "No, I am not trying to get you tipsy," he said in a gritty sounding voice.

"Hank!" Laura exclaimed, surprised and confused. "I wasn't accusing you of anything. I was teasing."

"Well, I'm not." His amber eyes blazed into hers. "I intend to make love with you tonight, Laura, and I don't want any questions later of whether or not you were fully aware of what you were doing."

The tension that had diminished during dinner slammed back into Laura. Despair swept through her. By exerting sheer willpower, she kept a crushing sense of defeat from showing. Her head snapped up; her voice was cool. "You're taking a lot for granted, Hank." Bitterness tinged her tone. "I was so hoping you were different from the other men I've dated and wouldn't expect me to pay with sexual favors for the meal provided."

"What!" Hank jumped up, knocking his chair to the floor with a crash. "What in hell are you saying?" His expression savage, he circled the table to her.

Frightened by the violence emanating from him, Laura cringed, but verbally lashed out, "Isn't that the way it's usually done in today's 'equal everything' society?"

"Damn you." Hank's voice was rough, yet the hands that grasped her shoulders to lift her from her chair were amazingly gentle. "You actually believe... Payment!" He was so angry he sputtered. "Dammit, Laura! I could shake you!" He did—directly into an embrace. "Payment... Oh, God, Laura." His voice was lost as he pressed his lips to her temple.

Expecting a violent eruption, Laura trembled at his display of tenderness. Feeling the tremor in her slender body, Hank tightened his arms convulsively around her.

"I won't hurt you," he murmured against her hair. "Laura, honey, I swear I'll never hurt you."

"You frightened me." Her voice was little more than a faint whisper.

"I'm sorry."

"For an instant I—" Laura's breath caught "—I really thought you were going to strike me."

"Strike you?" Hank's entire body tightened. "Good Lord!" He loosened his hold just enough to allow her to look up at him. His eyes glittered with inner fury. "Have you been struck by a man before?" His voice was chillingly soft.

All the moisture evaporated in Laura's mouth. The Hank she was staring at held very little resemblance to the Hank who had earlier fumbled with a hot loaf of bread. This man looked positively lethal. Laura swallowed and attempted to defuse the time bomb holding her with taut arms. "A slap," she admitted. "An-and really only a light slap." Her attempt at pacification failed. Hank's eyes narrowed.

"His name," he demanded in a too soft tone.

"Hank, it's no longer impor—"

"I want his name," he insisted.

"Why?"

His smile sent a finger of ice down her spine. "Why do you suppose?"

Laura could actually feel the color drain from her face. "You... Hank, you can't!" she cried in protest.

"Oh, I won't kill him," he assured her. "I won't even break him." His voice lowered to a hair-raising purr. "I'll only bend him a little."

"No!" Appalled, Laura strained against his embrace.

"Yes!" The muscles in his arms locked, holding her captive. "He struck you, Laura. Now, dammit, tell me his name!"

Compressing her lips, she shook her head in obstinate refusal. "It no longer matters, Hank. It happened a long time ago."

"How long?"

"Hank, this is ridiculous!"

He was adamant. "How long?"

Recognizing defeat, Laura gave up the fight. "Over five years," she answered on a sigh.

Hank looked astounded. "You haven't been with a man in over five years?"

Pride lent a sharpness to her voice. "I haven't *been* with a man in over ten years!"

His expression of astonishment expanded into sheer incredulity. "You're kidding?"

The look she leveled at him was all the answer he required.

"You're not kidding!" Hank blinked. "Well, I'll be damned," he murmured in bemusement.

Laura laughed; she couldn't help it. His confused expression was comical. But the laughter caught in her throat when she noticed masculine satisfaction and sudden arousal revealed in his eyes. "What are you thinking?" she asked suspiciously.

"That I'm going to be very careful not to hurt you," he replied, easing a hand to her face to stroke her cheek with one finger.

Laura shivered. "Hurt me?" she repeated in a near croak. "In...what way?"

"You know very well what way." He lowered his head as he answered.

Laura felt his moist breath caress her mouth on his last word. Without conscious thought, she parted her lips for him. Hank made an inarticulate sound deep in his throat, an exciting sound, part growl, part groan.

"Laura." He murmured her name as his mouth claimed hers.

Laura was floating, her senses swaying to the rhythmic movement of his mouth on hers. She was almost lost in a mist of gathering sensuality... almost. The urgency of his kiss pierced the haze clouding her mind, allowing a cold blast of uncertainty to rush in to clear her senses. Avoiding the play of his tongue to engage in an erotic duel with hers, she turned her head, withdrawing her mouth from his.

"Hank, please," she pleaded breathlessly. "I've got to go. It's getting late."

"Oh, come on, Laura." Impatience flashed across his face and colored his voice. "You're an adult, not a kid."

In a strange way, Laura was feeling much more a kid than an adult at that moment, and a very inexperienced kid, at that. "I know," she said. "But they'll worry."

"Who are they?"

"Megan," she answered. "And Ruth, my housekeeper."

Hank arched his brows in an imperious manner. "You must account to your housekeeper?"

"No, of course not!" Laura exclaimed. "But—"

"Megan," he interjected.

"Yes, Megan."

Hank sighed but tightened his hold on her. "Are you and Megan playing some sort of role reversal game?"

"Don't be ridiculous!" she denied angrily.

"I'm ridiculous?" Hank laughed grimly. "Honey, you are thirty-nine years old and telling me you must rush home at—" he shot a glance at his wrist watch "—10:11 at night." He laughed again. "And you accuse me of being ridiculous?"

Laura bit her lip. "I'm sorry, but I did explain yesterday about Megan."

"And I understood," Hank said. "That's why we had dinner here, instead of in a restaurant, where they probably wouldn't have overcrisped the bread."

"The bread was delicious!" Laura objected.

Hank shook his head. "That's beside the point, and you know it. Does Megan know you're here with me?"

"You know she doesn't."

"Right." Hank drew a tantalizing line along her cheek with his fingertip. "Then why the panic?"

Laura lowered her lashes. "I'm scared, Hank."

His arms flexed, crushing her breasts against the hard wall of his chest. "I swore I wouldn't hurt you, Laura." His voice was low and intense.

"And I believe you . . . but . . ." Her voice failed.

"But?" he prompted.

She glanced up quickly, then as quickly looked down again. "It's been so long for me." She hesitated, then explained in a rush. "I'm out of practice."

"Out of . . ." Hank's voice got lost in the laughter spilling from his throat. "Is that all?" He lowered one arm to her thighs, then swung her up into his arms. "In that case, let's find a comfortable spot and practice together."

The comfortable spot he found was the king-size bed in his bedroom. Hank lowered her to the bed fully clothed, then stretched out beside her. Laura's body was stiff from the combined effects of excitement and nervousness.

Handling her like delicate crystal, Hank drew her trembling body close to the protective strength of his. "There's nothing to be afraid of, Laura," he murmured, skimming his lips over the trail his finger had blazed on her cheek. "I'm not going to force any issues here or do anything that doesn't please you."

Slowly, as Hank whispered reassurances to her, stroked her arm lightly with one hand and caressed her face with feather-soft kisses, then tension eased from Laura's rigid form to be replaced by an unfurling warmth and need deep inside her. As her growing pliancy became obvious, his brushing kisses drew ever nearer to her mouth. She sighed when his lips teased the corner of hers and, moaning softly, turned to capture his mouth with her own.

Hank kissed her sweetly, without demand, again and again before releasing her mouth and raising his head a fraction. "Does that please you?" he murmured.

Laura smiled. "Yes, it pleases me very much."

"Would you like to advance to the next plateau of practice?"

Her breath caught, but she whispered, "Yes."

Hank's kiss began as sweetly as before, then slowly the sweetness was replaced by the increasing heat of his hunger. He drew her lower lip into his mouth to gently suck on it and softly sank his teeth into the sensitive inner flesh in an electrifying love bite. Then he slowly inserted his tongue into her mouth and paused, waiting for her reaction.

Laura responded at once. Curling her arms around his neck, she arched her body into his and stroked his tongue with her own. Fire raced through her body and converged in her abdomen. Her fingers speared through his shaggy mane; her nails lightly scored his scalp; her soft body molded itself to the unrelenting hardness of his. Hank responded by deepening the kiss and raking the moist cavern of her mouth.

His breathing was ragged and uneven when he raised his head again. "Does that please you?" he asked.

"Yes," Laura breathed, "but . . ."

Hank frowned. "I didn't hurt you, did I?"

She moved her head against the pillow.

"Then what?"

Laura grasped for a way to convey her desire, then murmured tentatively, "It's a little warm in here, isn't it?"

He drew his breath in with a hiss, then demoralized her completely with his slow sexy smile. "What do you suggest we do about it?" he murmured in a devilish teasing tone.

Laura could barely breathe, but she forced herself to answer. "Undress," she said unsteadily.

Hank rewarded her with a quick hard kiss. "You amaze me," he complimented, rolling away from her.

"In what way?" Laura asked, crawling from the bed to stand before him.

He shrugged and reached for the top button of her blouse. "I didn't think you'd have the courage to tell me."

Laura tilted her chin. "I have plenty of courage," she informed him with more than a hint of asperity.

"Do you?" Amusement laced his voice.

She shivered as his palms smoothed the silky material over her shoulders and down her arms. "Yes. I never said I was a coward. I said I was—"

"Out of practice," Hank finished for her, bending to slide the skirt down her body.

Laura was suddenly afraid her quivering legs would fold sending her crashing into a heap at his feet. "Yes," she replied on a sharply expelled breath. She nearly cried out in response to the thrill he sent streaking through her by gliding his palms up her thighs, over her buttocks and upward to her breasts. A deft flick of his fingers dispensed with the front clasp of her bra. The filmy scrap of material floated noiselessly to the floor. The thrill intensified inside her as he examined her from head to toe with narrowed intent eyes.

"You're beautiful." His voice was low, sandpaper harsh. "And you've got gorgeous legs."

Laura felt a burst of pleasure radiate through her trembling body. Her throat went dry. Her eyes grew moist. "I..." She had to pause to swallow. "Thank you. I...think you're beautiful, too."

"How can you tell?" he asked chidingly.

Laura blinked the moisture from her eyes. "I don't understand. What do you mean?"

His broad hands encircled her waist. "Being out of practice, I suppose you haven't noticed the disparity here," he said mildly.

She frowned in confusion. "Disparity? What do you mean?"

Hank's voice held a promise of laughter. "I'm the only one practicing undressing."

"Oh!" Laura gasped. "You want me to undress you?"

His laughter lived up to its promise. "It's only fair, you know," he said when the laughter subsided. "While I'm practicing on you, you can practice on me."

Laura reached out to comply, drawing another burst of laughter from him with a muttered, "Somehow I'm convinced you're not nearly as out of practice at this as I am."

By the time he settled her once more on the large bed, Hank's laughter had long since melted in the heat shimmering between them, and Laura had revised her compliment to him. In her stated opinion, he wasn't merely beautiful, he was blatantly magnificent.

His skin was smooth and warm to the touch as he slid his body against hers. Shivering in the heat, Laura stroked his warm skin and quivered in response to the tremor that rippled through his corded muscles.

"I like the way you practice," he murmured against her breast. "Practice some more," he invited, flicking his tongue over the hardening crest.

Laura cried aloud at the sensation that zigzagged from her breast to the most feminine part of her. In reaction, she simultaneously raked her nails along the curve of his spine and arched her back to allow him better access to her breasts.

"More practice," Hank demanded, closing his teeth around one crest.

She didn't have to be asked twice. Loving the feel of him, Laura explored freely, stroking, caressing every inch of him she could reach. Murmuring shocking exciting words, Hank embarked on an exploration of his own, kissing, nipping her body everywhere—everywhere!—until Laura felt she'd shatter from sheer pleasure.

"More," he growled as he moved up to plunder her mouth. "Full practice."

Laura understood. Slowly, glorying in his sharply indrawn breath, she clasped him, cradled him in her soft palms. Hank's tongue thrust into her mouth again and again, deeper and yet deeper, in an erotic imitation of a more complete possession. Her too long denied passion swirled out of control and, wildly aroused, she arched her body in a silent plea of unity.

The feel of his lightly haired thighs rubbing against the sensitive inner skin of hers created tiny tremors deep inside her. Her breath was almost nonexistent. Never before in her life had Laura experienced anything quite like the coiling tension building within her, not even with the man she had married. Never had she needed her husband as she so desperately needed Hank inside of her.

"The ultimate practice." With those words, Hank joined his body to hers.

His penetration immediately ripped the fabric of tension, releasing a pulsating flood of pleasure in Laura. Gasping, she rode the wave of ecstasy, but as it waned she turned her face to the pillow and moaned, "I'm sorry, I couldn't wait for you."

Hank had stilled inside her when the explosion caught her. Leaning to her, he gently nipped at her earlobe. "Was it good?" he asked in a husky voice.

"Wonderful," Laura admitted, "but you didn't..."

"I can wait." Hank outlined her jaw with the tip of his tongue.

"Wait for what?" Laura turned her head, and his tongue slipped into her mouth. Within seconds his erotic play sent liquid fire racing through her veins.

"The next time," he answered when he released her mouth to seek her breast.

Once again the white-hot electricity shot through Laura. In stunned amazement she felt the tension begin to coil. Hank moved his hips in a slow rhythmic cadence. Her breath grew harsh, then shallow. His cadence increased. She clasped his hips with her thighs. His thrust went deep, then deeper. She arched her body, demanding more. Her palms felt his slick skin. His hands grasped her hips, lifting her.

"Yes. Oh, yes!" Laura wasn't even aware of crying her pleasure aloud. "Hank! Hank!"

"Now, love!" Hank's fingers dug into her flesh. "Now!"

Laura splintered, scattering into a million shards of pulsating exquisite pleasure. Then slowly the pieces reformed into a single exhausted unit. A long sigh whispered through her parched lips.

"I want to die," she declared.

"I think I did," Hank muttered against her breast.

A soft smile curving her lips, Laura closed her eyes. Her smile deepened as she recalled the conversation she'd had with Ginnie yesterday afternoon. If Ginnie only knew, Laura mused dreamily. Her cage had been well and truly rattled! She snuggled into the hard warmth of the cage rattler and was immediately asleep.

Hank's movement woke her. She felt empty, abandoned. She parted her lips to protest, but the protest was forgotten when he drew her into his arms.

"What time is it?" she mumbled around a yawn.

"Time for good little grandmothers to be in bed." His voice held a smile.

"I am in bed," Laura pointed out sleepily.

Hank laughed. "I mean your own bed." He was quiet a moment. When he continued there was a note of hope in his voice. "Or were you considering spending the night with me?"

Laura sighed. "You know I can't do that, Hank."

He moved with restless impatience. "I know nothing of the kind. Dammit, Laura, you're a mature woman. Who you choose to sleep with is your business."

Laura felt a twinge—of anger? Remorse? She didn't know, and at that moment she was too tired to sort out her feelings. She pressed her palms lightly against his chest and felt a tingle from the contact with his skin and wiry hair. The tingle spread up her arms at the evidence of the responsive tremor that shuddered through him. Her heart skipped a beat when he caught her chin with his hand and tilted her face up to his.

"I need a kiss."

She fought a melting sensation. "I must go, Hank."

"Just one more . . . kiss."

Laura knew full well the portent of his brief hesitation, just as she knew one kiss would not be enough for either one of them. She knew, and offered her mouth to him anyway.

This time their lovemaking was sweet and tender, slow and easy. Until near the climax. Then it became hot and demanding, fast and desperate—and altogether wonderful.

Afterward Laura absolutely refused to let herself fall asleep, because she knew if she allowed herself to drift off, she'd be out until morning. But she rested, she had no choice; Hank's loving had drained her completely.

Another half hour elapsed before Laura felt strong enough to drag her sated body from the bed. While she availed herself of Hank's shower and then dressed, he made her a reviving cup of coffee. In between sips of the steaming brew, she stripped and remade the bed while Hank used the shower. As she smoothed the bedspread over the large bed, it struck Laura how natural it seemed to be there with him.

The thought occupied Laura's mind as Hank drove her back to the subdivision for her car. And, since he was unusually quiet during the ride, she followed the train of thought to its conclusion.

Why should being with Hank feel natural and somehow right? Laura asked herself, stealing a sideways glance at his attractive profile. On consideration, she'd have thought that after making love for the first time in so many years, she'd now be feeling embarrassed and awkward and relieved to be going home. Instead, she felt natural, fulfilled, replete and disappointed at the need to leave his side. Odd.

"What are you brooding about?" Hank's low voice interrupted her thoughts.

"I'm not brooding," she denied, turning with the confines of the safety belt to look at him.

He slanted a dry look at her. "Are you suffering regret for what happened?"

Her smile was soft. "No, Hank. I'm neither suffering nor regretting . . . anything."

"Good." He flashed a grin. "Because it's going to happen again."

Laura matched his grin. "Anytime soon?" she asked audaciously.

Hank's laughter boomed inside the car. "Tomorrow night?" He matched her audacity.

She would not be outaudacioused. "Shall I pack a toothbrush?"

"Yes," he said at once. Then, "No, dammit!" He cursed as he pulled the car to a stop beside hers. His chest heaved in a sigh as he turned to face her. "My brother's coming to stay with me for a while," Hank explained. "He'll arrive sometime Saturday. I don't want to run the risk of him showing up early and walking in on us."

"No," Laura agreed. "I don't think I'd enjoy that."

"I'm certain you wouldn't," he replied cryptically. "Will I see you here at the house tomorrow?"

Laura nodded. "Yes."

Hank drummed his fingers on the steering wheel. "Think up some excuse to be away for the night."

Laura was startled. "But . . . if you're expecting your brother . . . why?"

"I'll think of something."

Seven

The something Hank thought of was an oversize bed with a black-lacquered headboard.

It was late in the afternoon when Laura arrived at the model house. Unlike the previous day, she didn't stop to admire the subdivision or contemplate the thought and planning that had gone into the development. It was raining, hard. Huddling beneath a small folding umbrella, she dashed for the front door, silently hoping she'd again find it unlocked. It was. After setting the open umbrella to dry on the flag-stone floor in the foyer, she draped her raincoat on the banister then, obeying a compulsive urge to begin in the master suite, mounted the stairs.

Laura stopped dead in her tracks in the bedroom doorway, her astonished gaze riveted on the bed, which took up a fair portion of the spacious room. But her amazement didn't stem as much from the bed, which had seemingly materialized out of thin air overnight, as it did from the simple fact that the bed was a near duplicate to the one she had admired in a furniture showroom that very morning. On the spot she had decided the bed was perfect for the house and Hank. And, even though the bed had sported a shocking price tag, she had planned to discuss the purchase of it with Hank this afternoon.

Incredible!

Wondering where Hank had found the twin to the bed that had immediately caught her own fancy, Laura slowly entered the room. Her expression a mixture of bemusement and disbelief, she approached the bed. A suggestive red spread had been neatly smoothed over the mattress and pillows. Reaching out tentatively, she grasped the spread and pulled it away. A whispered "Oh" breathed through her parted lips. Beneath the spread, the bed had been expertly made with shimmering satin sheets.

Dropping the spread as if it had actually burned her fingers, Laura raised her hand to her mouth to stifle a burst of appreciative laughter. The bedding was so blatant, so obvious, so...so damn sexy!

"Tickles your funny bone, does it?"

Hand clamped to her mouth, Laura spun around at the sound of Hank's voice. Not trusting herself to speak without choking on her laughter, she nodded in response.

Pushing away from his now familiar pose against the frame, Hank strolled toward her. His chest heaved in a dramatic-sounding sigh. "Pity. Your funny bone wasn't quite the area I was aiming for." The amusement glowing from his amber eyes belied the note of disappointment in his voice.

"Where—" Laura had to pause to collect herself before asking "—where did you find it?"

Her eyes widened when he mentioned the show-room she'd visited that morning. "I couldn't resist," he added. "I could just *see* it in this room."

"I could, too!" she exclaimed, then explained that she had also had reason to be in that particular show-room. "It just seemed to cry out your name to me."

"Hmm." Hank angled a breath-stealing smile at her. "You think I'm red, black and sexy looking, do you?"

Laura managed a prim expression. "As I recall, the bed in the showroom was made up with pastel-colored sheets." She prudently refrained from admitting that she had thought the light shades unsuitable for the bed, and indeed had imagined it draped in the more dramatic red.

"Yeah." Hank grimaced. "Looked kind'a blah and uninteresting to me." His grimace evolved into a suggestive grin. "Wanna try it out?"

"Hank!" Laura was startled and a little shocked...and entirely too enthralled and excited by the prospect. "It's broad daylight!"

"Sounds like fun to me." Reaching out, he caught her by the waist and drew her body into intimate con-tact with his. "I've been picturing you sprawled na-ked in the sunlight on that bed ever since it was delivered around noon," he murmured against her slightly parted lips. "My imagination has been driv-ing me crazy all afternoon."

His teasing mouth was driving her crazy at that moment. Her sense of excitement was swiftly overcoming her sense of shock—and even her sense of propriety. She was there to work; his clothes were covered with a layer of gritty dust; his men were still on the job somewhere in the subdivision. Suddenly Laura didn't care about any of the cautioning reminders that flashed through her mind. She was burning up inside. Only Hank's mouth could quench the fire.

Raising her hands, she clasped his head to still the teasing movement of his lips brushing back and forth over hers. Rising up on her toes, Laura pressed her parted mouth to his. Instead of quenching her inner fire, Hank's kiss sent it raging out of control. He wrenched a hungry moan from her with a wicked flick of his tongue and responded to the low sound by sweeping her up into his arms.

"God, Laura," he groaned into her mouth. "After last night, I can't believe how much I still want you."

Her arms clasped around his neck, Laura trembled with the realization of her equal need for him. Yet, a small portion of her resisted the inappropriateness of their intent. Feeling she should, she began to protest. "Hank, I really think we should wait until—"

"I can't remember ever wanting any woman as badly as I want you, now, here...continually."

His reluctantly muttered confession vanquished doubt, protest and the small portion of resistance inside Laura. She didn't care that she wasn't working; she didn't care that her sensitized skin felt every tiny grain of dust on his clothes and body; she didn't care that his men were somewhere in the vicinity. All Laura knew and cared about was being with Hank, holding him close, sharing with him the most intimate embrace experienced by lovers.

"No," she murmured in protest when he set her down beside the bed and released her. Reflexively, she tightened her arms around his neck. "Don't go away."

"I'm not going anywhere," Hank reassured her. He grasped her shoulders and turned her around.

"Hank?" Laura moved to face him again, but he held her still with her back towards him.

"Indulge me," he said, raising his hands to the twist in her hair. "I want to see you, all of you, in daylight, with your hair unbound and spread out on the pillow." He slid the anchoring pins from her hair as he spoke.

Laura shivered. The night before, though the twist in her hair had loosened and errant strands had slipped free to lie in long curls at her nape, the mass had remained held in place by the wire pins. Her shiver intensified as she felt her thick hair tumble to her shoulders. For some inexplicable reason, the thought of her hair wildly tangled around her on the bed seemed the height of abandonment.

"That's better." Hank slid his fingers through the long strands of her hair as he turned her to face him again. His eyes glowed with a sensual inner light. "In fact, it's better than better." His fingers slowly combed through her hair from her scalp to the curled tips that swirled around her shoulders. "Beautiful," he murmured in a husky response to the tactile sensation. "I wanted to touch your hair the moment I walked into your home and saw it."

The expression on his face stole her breath away. Suddenly abandonment held an overwhelming allure for Laura. Hank smiled. She melted. Her arms felt heavy, languid as she raised her hands to his chest. Her fingers trembled on the first button at the base of his throat.

"You want to see all of me in daylight, too," Hank said on an indrawn breath. "Don't you?" He trailed his hands from her hair to the top button of her blouse.

"Yes." Laura's voice was the merest whisper.

Then all was silent as they stood beside the blatantly suggestive bed, their concentration centered on the tiny buttons of her silk blouse and the more sturdy buttons of his cotton work shirt. Laura's breathing grew shallow and irregular as her trembling fingers exposed the broad expanse of his smooth tanned chest. And she could hear the uneven rasp of Hank's breath as his hands gently parted the silky material of her blouse to reveal her small breasts inadequately concealed by the wispy lace of her bra. The touch of cool air on her heated flesh induced a measure of trepidation in Laura. She had to moisten her lips in order to convey her sudden concern.

"Your men are still around. What if someone should come into the house?"

Hank paused in the act of tugging her blouse from the waistband of her skirt. "No one would dare." His smile softened the arrogant sound of his voice.

The statement still hung in the air when a call from the foyer shattered the aura of sensuality surrounding them.

"Yo, Hank! You in here?"

"I'll fire him," Hank muttered before angling his head to shout, "Yeah, Dave, what's your problem?"

The spell was definitely broken. Laura was rebuttoning her blouse before the answer reverberated through the empty structure.

"There's a young couple out here wants to talk to you about buying the house."

Even with a foot of space separating them, Laura could feel Hank stiffen, reflecting the tension suddenly gripping her own quivering muscles.

Buy the house! This house? Hank's house? *Our* house! The thoughts crowded into Laura's mind all at once and united in a single silent cry of protest. *No!*

"Okay, tell them I'll be there in a minute, Dave."

Hank's reply had the same effect on Laura as a pin piercing a balloon. She felt deflated, and a draining sense of weariness overwhelmed her. Stiffening her spine to keep her shoulders from drooping, she met the glittering gaze he turned to her and willed her tone to remain unaffected.

"Well," she said with deceptive calm, "I may very soon be redundant."

Hank had started out of the room, refastening his shirt buttons as he walked. Her remark stopped him cold, and he glanced over his shoulder, a frown drawing his dark brows into a straight line. "What are you talking about?"

"The young couple waiting to see you," she explained. "If they decide to buy the house, you certainly won't need a decorator."

"They're not going to buy the house," he said, turning to face her.

"How do you know that?" Laura despaired of the tremor in her voice that betrayed her facade of composure.

Hank finished buttoning his shirt, then planted his big hand on his hips before answering. "Because they can't buy a house that's not available," he said distinctly. "And this house is *not* for sale."

"Oh." Laura felt the gathering weight of depression begin to lift. "Why isn't it?"

"Why?" He glanced at the bed, then at her. Then he smiled. "Because this place is ours...exclusively."

His reply set her spirit soaring. Her brilliant smile relayed her feeling to him. He took a step toward her; she held up a hand, palm out. "They're waiting. You'd better go." His hesitation was the nicest of compliments.

Hank stared at her a moment, then he exhaled a rueful-sounding sigh. "Right." As if afraid that unless he moved at once he wouldn't move at all, he strode to the door and pulled it open. But once more he paused to slant a smile at her. "I do like your hair down," he said softly. Then he was gone, gently shutting the door behind him.

Laura's burst of laughter held a new youthful note of freedom. The man was wicked, she mused, raising her hand to touch the unfettered locks brushing her shoulders, but he was *wonderfully* wicked. Laughing softly, she knelt to retrieve the hairpins and her handbag from the floor, then headed for the bathroom. Wearing her hair down for Hank was one thing. But Laura had work to do in the house, and allowing others to see her looking disheveled and unprofessional was something else altogether.

In exactly the same way she had stopped short in the bedroom doorway earlier, Laura came to an abrupt halt when she opened the bathroom door, her eyes wide as she took stock of the changes Hank had made. By itself, the room was attractive, if rather stark. Now it looked lived-in.

Red and black towels had been hung neatly over the glass rods mounted on the black-and-gold marbled mirror wall. Small red drip mats had been placed next to the shower and inset tub to protect the plush black-and-white flecked wall-to-wall carpet on the floor. Hank's shaving kit and assorted toiletries were placed to the side of one sink on the brazen red double-sink vanity. A black-handled toothbrush was the sole occupant of the holder mounted on the wall between the sinks. But, most surprising of all was the large feathery-leafed Boston fern hanging from a ceiling bracket near the wide frosted-glass window.

"Lived-in and intimate," Laura announced, laughing again as she moved into the room. After scattering the pins on the smooth vanity surface, she unzipped her bag and withdrew her makeup case and a small brush. Wielding the brush, she smoothed the tangles from her hair and folded the tamed strands into a classic twist at the back of her head. Holding the hair in place with one hand, she glanced into the mirror while reaching for a pin with the other.

Laura barely recognized the woman reflected in the mirror. Automatically inserting the pins into her hair, she studied the image staring back at her. The woman looked younger, less work harried and a lot less tense than the image Laura was accustomed to confronting.

Could one night—half a night, precisely—with Hank really have wrought such an obvious change in her? The question was rhetorical, Laura knew, for she felt the change inside as well as on the surface. After the exhausting intensity of their lovemaking the night before, she *should* be feeling ragged and played out. Yet, quite the opposite was true. She was feeling more alive, more vibrant than she had in years.

Fortunately, that morning Megan had been too rushed and Ruth too busy to question Laura when she calmly informed them that she would be away overnight due to business reasons.

"New client?" Megan asked distractedly, gulping down her juice and glancing at the clock.

"Yes." Laura abhorred deception and was relieved at being able to answer truthfully. Hank was in fact a new client. She was even more relieved when Megan accepted her response and didn't pursue the subject.

"Do you want me to call Brooke and Don and tell them we won't be able to make it to play bridge tomorrow night?" Megan asked as she slid her chair away from the table.

"No, of course not." Laura shook her head; she had completely forgotten about the date. "I'll be home in plenty of time."

"Okay," Megan said, heading for the door. "I'm outta here. See you tomorrow."

Ruth had frowned when she placed a poached egg on diet wheat toast on the table in front of Laura, but her only comment had been, "Bit unusual, isn't it?"

"Uh-huh," Laura had murmured over the rim of her coffee cup while thinking that, at least for her, what she was doing was a lot more than a bit unusual.

Of course, Laura hadn't felt obligated to mention anything at all to Ginnie. And yet, throughout the day she had noticed the younger woman observing her, her expression thoughtful and speculative.

Gazing into the mirror, Laura now felt she knew why Ginnie had looked so strangely at her. In truth, she actually looked different than she had yesterday. And she certainly felt different!

But how exactly did she feel? Laura mused, frowning at her reflection as she poked the last pin into place. That was definitely Laura Seaton frowning back at her from the mirror. And yet, it was a different Laura Seaton. But in what way had she changed?

Laura blinked, startled by the answer that immediately sprang to mind. She looked like a woman fulfilled and happy! Shaking her head in wonderment, she turned away from the mirror. Damn! She hadn't even realized she felt unfulfilled and unhappy!

Laughing softly at her thoughts, Laura told herself to get out of the bathroom and get to work. Heaven alone knew when the unpredictable cause of her physical and emotional metamorphosis might appear.

Hank stood staring into space long after the obviously disappointed young couple had driven away from the site. Though the rain had subsided in intensity, it was still falling. Hank barely noticed it. His thoughts were centered on his own suddenly incomprehensible actions. In comparison to the thoughts and emotions he was attempting to sort through, rain-soaked clothing was of little importance.

The snap decision he'd made concerning the house didn't bother him, probably because it really hadn't been a snap decision at all. Hank had a gut feeling that somewhere deep in his subconscious, he had known that since seeing Laura in the house, he would be unable to sell the model home.

Had it only been two days? he marveled. Things were happening too fast, the relationship between them was accelerating too swiftly. Hank felt unsure, off balance. He didn't appreciate the feeling.

But, contrarily, he didn't want to slow things down, either. While logic advised him to put some distance between himself and Laura, emotion demanded he get closer to her. The mere idea that he might run the risk of losing her by suggesting a cooling-off period, sent an unfamiliar cold fear streaking down his spine, Hank was even less appreciative of that feeling.

And so, there he was, standing in the chilly spring rain, experiencing the uncomfortable sensation of being trapped between a rock and a hard place.

The very last thing he wanted was a commitment—that is, Hank had believed that the last thing he wanted was a commitment. Of course, that had been on the previous Sunday, and now it was Friday.

Five days. Two days short of a full week. He couldn't build a house in five days. Was it really possible to build a relationship in that amount of time? Hank asked himself. Or was he simply two bricks short a full load?

How many times did a man have to be scorched before he learned to be wary of a flame? he chided himself. Didn't he consider himself to be a reasonably intelligent man? He had been more than scorched; he had been seared to the depths of his emotions by one woman. And his younger brother had been charred by another. While the embers were still hot and glowing, Hank had vowed he would never be as much as singed again. Yet here he was, standing in the rain while his intellect warred with his emotions over another woman.

The smile that twisted Hank's mouth was wry and self-derisive. If he had any sense, he thought, he'd pull on an asbestos suit and back away, out of reach of the fire, before he woke up some morning to discover he had been emotionally consumed by the conflagration.

But the flame named Laura was mesmerizing, and Hank could visualize paradise deep within the blaze. With a shrug, he angled his squared jaw arrogantly. He wouldn't back off; he wouldn't slow down; he wouldn't quit. He wanted Laura, wanted to be with her, laugh with her, love with her. Period. He was more aware than most of the risks involved. For Laura, Hank was willing to take them.

Turning, he gazed long and hard at the house, picturing the woman inside. Then a smile lightened the austerity of his expression, and he made yet another snap decision. He was going to take Laura dancing. But first he needed to change out of his soggy clothes. Spinning around he headed for the van, thinking, what the hell, if he was going to play at all, he might just as well go for the whole nine yards!

Hank was whistling softly as he pushed the key into the ignition.

* * *

Where was Hank? Laura had grown familiar with the query during the seemingly endless hours since his departure. She had become fearful of the answer. Had he changed his mind about selling the house and become engrossed in the details attendant to the purchase of a property?

In an attempt to avoid the speculation, Laura had filled the intervening hours productively. Although the questions and doubts buzzed inside her head, she had pages full of notes, itemizing the furnishings she envisioned for every room down to the type of potted plants that were best suited to each room's light.

She had worked hard, and she was hungry. So, where was Hank? Closing her briefcase with an impatient-sounding smack, Laura started for the steps. She was halfway down the stairs when the front door opened and Hank walked in. The sight of him arrested her descent.

Dressed in dusty work clothes, Hank looked wonderful. Attired in a brown suit and pale yellow shirt that closely matched the gold-flecked color of his hair, Hank's effect on her was stunning.

"You changed." Instantly aware of stating the obvious, she frowned and asked, "Why did you change?"

His steps measured, Hank crossed the foyer and started up the stairs toward her. "Because I was dirty and wet," he answered as he mounted the steps. "But mostly because I want to take you out to dinner and then dancing," he finished as he came to a stop on the step below the one she was standing on.

"Dancing!" Laura exclaimed on a laugh. "I haven't been dancing in years."

"Then it's long past time you—"

"Oh, Hank, I can't, we can't!" Laura cried, interrupting him. "You know we can't."

The shimmer of anticipation disappeared from his gleaming amber eyes, leaving them looking as flat and dull as an unwashed stone. "Megan." Hank's tone lacked inflection.

Laura felt as badly as she had on the occasions when she'd had to deny her daughters a longed-for treat. "Yes. I'm sorry."

"Yeah." He exhaled deeply. Without another word, he pivoted and started down the stairs.

Alarm snaked through Laura. "Where are you going?" Her cry stopped him at the door.

Hank slanted a look at her over his shoulder. "Where else? For dinner." Suddenly his eyes began to glow, and he flashed a devastating grin. "Only this time, instead of the hard floor, we'll have our picnic in bed." He arched his brows imperiously. "Any comments?"

Laura gave him a long cool stare, then a slow enticing smile. "Yes. Don't get anything messy."

Savoring his bark of laughter, she stared at the door for a moment after he closed it behind him. Then an idea sparked that galvanized her into action. Setting her briefcase on the step, she rushed down the remaining stairs and out of the house. A few minutes later she rushed in again, carrying her overnight case.

After a quick shower, Laura slipped into a filmy chiffon negligee, which she had hurriedly bought while supposedly on her lunch break. She kept her makeup to the barest minimum, but brushed her hair until it gleamed. She heard him pull up outside as she dabbed perfume on her wrists and between her breasts. She heard his tread on the stairs as she shut the bathroom door. She was standing by the bed, waiting for him, when he walked into the room. The stunned expression that washed over his face when he saw her made all her frantic activity worth the effort. The two words he breathed were all that were necessary to still her fluttering uncertainty.

"God, Laura!"

"You're not angry about not being able to go out for dinner and dancing?" she asked, needing reassurance.

Hank's stunned expression dissolved in his slow smile. "No, I'm not angry about dinner." He set the two white fast-food restaurant bags he was holding to one side, and shrugged out of his suit jacket before moving toward her.

Watching him, his measured pace, the look in his eyes, Laura felt anticipation unfurl in the pit of her stomach. The careless way he tossed his jacket onto the foot of the bed defined his intentions and increased the expectancy that was humming through her. Distracted, excited, she said the first coherent thought that came to mind.

"Dinner will get cold."

"I won't," Hank purred, reaching for her. "And, as for the dancing," he continued, drawing her to him as he came to a stop, "I have a much more satisfying form of exercise in mind." Sliding one hand into her hair at her nape, he tangled his fingers in the strands and tugged her face up to meet his descending mouth.

"It begins with this basic mouth-to-mouth movement."

Hank's demonstration was graphic and comprehensive, involving not only mouths but teeth and tongues and murmured moans of mutual enjoyment. Dinner was forgotten, overshadowed by a deeper richer hunger. They fed from each other's mouths with greedy intent. Reality receded . . . only the arousing realm of erotica existed.

The initial kiss evolved into two, then three, then Laura lost count. The pleasure went on and on, expanding, growing, spiraling through Laura until she couldn't think and didn't want to think. She felt weakened while quivering with sizzling energy. When the kiss finally ended and Hank lifted his mouth from hers, Laura was his, and he knew it as surely as she knew he was hers.

His breathing was labored, his voice was husky. "This is lovely," he said, fingering the gossamer negligee. "Let's get rid of it."

Laura wasn't shocked or even shy; she was eager to comply. As fine as it was, the chiffon was having a chafing effect against her sensitized skin. His broad hands stroked the garment from her flesh.

Unafraid and unashamed, Laura stood still and proud while Hank drank in her beauty with amber eyes shadowed by passion. When his darkened gaze returned to her eyes, she arched one delicate eyebrow and softly declared, "I think one of us is dreadfully overdressed."

First Hank smiled, then he chuckled, then he threw back his shaggy head and roared with delighted laughter. Swinging her into his arms, he held her in a crushing embrace. Laura could hear the laughter reverberating inside his broad chest. He kissed her, hard and openmouthed, making his laughter a moist, living part of her.

"You're fantastic," he said, leaning his head back to grin down at her.

"And you're still overdressed." Laura retorted.

"Not for long," he vowed. Laughing again, Hank swept her off her feet and, with calculated caution, tossed her onto the bed. "Now, pay attention," he warned, expertly flipping open the buttons on his shirt, "or you'll miss it."

Scrambling to her knees, Laura was extremely attentive. With unstudied sensuality she moistened her lips, which grew progressively dryer as each consecutive piece of clothing was discarded, revealing another portion of his magnificent body to her wide appreciative eyes. When at last he stood tall beside the bed, glorious in his nakedness, she raised her arms to him in a gesture both inviting and supplicating.

"If you continue to look at me like that," Hank groaned, moving onto the bed and drawing her into his arms, "it will be morning before you get your dinner."

Morning. That one word rang an alarm in Laura's bemused mind. "Morning!" she exclaimed, clasping his head to halt his obvious intention to capture her mouth. "Hank, are your men working tomorrow morning?"

"Yes, but not to worry," he murmured, gliding his hands around her rib cage and stroking the curve of her breasts with his long fingers. "They'll only be on the site till noon, and I left orders that no one was to enter this house.''

"But," Laura began, then gasped, "Oh!" as he slid his palms up and over her aching breasts. "You don't understand," she moaned, leaning into his cradling hands. "I left my car parked in front of the house. Someone is bound to recognize it!"

"No, love," he crooned, extending his fingers for a more extensive caress. "I parked your car in the garage when I returned from getting our dinner.''

Laura blinked in surprise, then sighed in response to the sensations his stroking fingers aroused deep inside her. "How did you do that?"

"What?" Hank chuckled. "This?" The tip of his finger brushed over the quivering crest of one breast.

Laura's eyelids felt weighted and too heavy to remain open; her breath came in shallow puffs. "No," she replied on a breathy whisper. "How did you manage to move the car without the key?"

"Don't ask," Hank advised, laughing softly as he took her down to the mattress.

Laura didn't. She no longer cared. He was there, loving her. Curling her arms around his neck, she loved him back.

Eight

——

Sometime after midnight, Laura discovered that she liked the taste of cold chicken nuggets washed down with tepid chenin blanc. Of course, by then, having successfully completed Hank's program of beneficial exercises, Laura was famished.

"Leave that until morning and come back to bed," Hank said, raising his arms high over his head in a luxurious stretch. He was sitting up, propped against the lacquered headboard, his naked body exposed from hipline to hairline.

The chiffon negligee swirling around her legs, Laura crossed the room to set the paper bags, now full of trash, next to the door. "It would have taken only a minute to carry this down to the kitchen and dump it in the trash compactor," she replied, frowning as she returned to bed.

"And it'll only take a minute in the morning. Besides, you're barefoot, and I'm getting lonely all alone in here." Hank patted the mattress beside his scarlet-draped hip.

"You're not getting lonely," she muttered with assumed asperity. "You're getting hor—"

"Laura Seaton! You *are* shocking." Hank's sharply indrawn breath interrupted her. Pulling her into his arms, he dragged her onto the bed and into an intimate embrace. "And you are so right," he confessed, giving her proof by settling her body on top of his.

Laura struggled with him—simply because it felt so good. An enticing smile curved her mouth when Hank gasped and clamped his hands on her hips to hold her still.

"Take pity, woman!" he groaned, arching his body convulsively into the softness of hers. "Do you have any idea what you're doing to me?"

Laura gave him a dry look and a long-suffering sigh. "Now I suppose you want to do *that* again."

Grinning wickedly, Hank slid his hands up her body, drawing off the negligee. "Oh, I insist," he whispered, and tossed the filmy gown to the floor.

Although their love play began with Laura straddling his reclining form, it was completed in a more traditional position, with Hank's arching body cradled within the silken circle of her thighs. They cried aloud simultaneously at the height of their ecstasy, and clung to each other, one body, one heart, one soul, as the storm of release subsided.

"You're more than wonderful," Hank murmured, holding her close and stroking her from waist to knee.

"You're more, much more, than I could ever have imagined in my wildest fantasies."

Closing her eyes against the sudden sting of tears, Laura curled closer to him and rubbed her cheek over his hair-rough chest. "You're not wonderful," she replied on a sigh. "You're magnificent, glorious, perfect."

"And you're delirious." Hank laughed and kissed the top of her head. "Delicious, but delirious. Go to sleep."

Laura didn't want to go to sleep; she didn't want to surrender one second of her time with Hank to unknowing unfeeling unconsciousness. Listening to him breathe, stroking his warm flesh, drawing the male scent of him deep into her senses, she fought off the swirling darkness of slumber long after Hank had succumbed to it. But it was an unequal contest, one she could not win. Inevitably, the wispy arms of slumber carried her away.

The unmistakable note of hunger in Hank's low voice brought her back.

"Wake up, Sleeping Beauty." The gentle pressure of his mouth on hers banished sleep from her mind. "It's nearly noon."

Laura moved supplely, loving the feel of his nakedness against her bare skin. She wasn't quite so beguiled by the information that slowly registered on her consciousness. "Noon!" Her eyes opened wide. "It can't be!"

Hank's eyes laughed into hers. "Why can't it?"

Laura frowned. Didn't he realize that she couldn't handle complex questions upon awakening? "Because I never sleep till noon," she mumbled.

His laughter spread from his eyes to his throat. The tender sound of it soothed her wake-up irritability. "You've achieved a first," he said, continuing to laugh softly. "And, if you'll sit up, I'll give you a second first."

He had lost her completely. A second first? Laura repeated to herself, dragging the red sheet with her as she wriggled into a sitting position. What in the world was a second first? Hank answered before she could assemble the words to ask the question aloud.

"Your very first morning cup of coffee in bed, in this house," he said, moving the steaming cup back and forth under her nose. "And, if I must say so myself, I do make a damn good cup of coffee."

Laura's nostrils flared; the brew smelled heavenly. Her mental facilities sharpening, she raised her eyes and gazed at him solemnly. "Are you going to give it to me?" she asked wryly. "Or are you getting your kicks by torturing me with it?"

"Oh, I'm going to give it to you." Flashing his most wicked grin yet, Hank handed the cup to her. "And, when I get my kicks, it won't be from playing games with coffee."

Before Hank, Laura had never engaged in the exciting intimacy of erotic wordplay. She had been too young and untutored with her husband—in fact, they'd both been pitifully inexperienced. And she'd been too circumspect and uptight to engage in any sensuality at all with the few men she'd dated since her husband's demise.

By being himself, Hank had opened a whole new world to her with his sensual teasing, a world in which a woman could be herself, express herself, enjoy herself to the limits of her personality. It was like coming of age, being set free. Laura loved it.

Maintaining her solemn expression, she lowered her gaze in a slow examination of his impressive form. Hank was naked to the waist. His tanned skin was burnished by the midday sunshine streaming in the windows. Beltless, his suit pants rode low on his hips, leaving little doubt in Laura's mind as to the absence of underpants beneath them. There was no doubt at all about the state of his arousal.

"You are insatiable," she accused, staring with unabashed fascination.

"Greedy, too," Hank admitted sardonically.

Laura wasn't altogether successful at containing a smile. "I guess you'd like me to hurry with my coffee?" Her inflection made the statement a question; her arched brows underlined it.

"Take your time," he said expansively. "I can wait."

"Indeed?" Swallowing the last of the reviving liquid, Laura slid down in the bed, set the cup on the floor, tossed the red sheet aside and held her arms out wide in invitation. "Well, I can't. So will you pease get out of those pants and get into this bed?"

For an instant Hank looked stunned. Then his pants slid to the floor and, with a whoop of delighted laughter, he launched himself onto the mattress beside her.

This time a new dimension was added to Laura's rapidly expanding experience of lovemaking. As little as one week ago, she wouldn't have believed it possible to make love and be rather silly at one and the same time. Yet, by example, Hank introduced her to the boundless possibilities available where uninhibited lovemaking was concerned.

Teasing, tickling, nipping each other, they laughed and romped over every inch of the large bed. It was only when their passion spiraled to an unbearable tension that laughter gave way to murmured sounds of mutual need.

For Laura, the descent from the ultimate edge of pleasure was soothed by Hank's caressing hands and whispered words.

"I am insatiable with you, Laura." His slightly parted lips brushed her cheek. "For now, my mind and body are at rest, replete and satisfied." His hand sculpted the curve of her breast. "I don't understand it." Puzzlement shaded his lowered voice. "I've always enjoyed sexual pleasure, but I can't remember ever being like this, not even as a teenager," he confided candidly. "With you, I've experienced the most intense satisfaction I've ever known. And yet it's never enough."

Flattered, flustered, misty-eyed, Laura lifted her head from his chest to gaze up at him. "I know, I feel the same way," she said, returning his candor. "I've never been this way...this abandoned...with a man, not even my husband. I feel like a different person when I'm with you."

"And do you like that person?" A faint expectant note shaded his low-pitched voice.

Laura didn't hesitate. "Yes, very much."

Hank smiled. "So do I. Very much."

"I'm glad." Laura snuggled closer to him, curling herself around the warm length of his body. A sigh of sheer contentment whispered through her lips and ruffled the springy hair on his chest. "I feel so good being here like this with you. I don't want to move, ever." She pressed her parted lips to his dewy skin and smiled when he shivered in response. A deeper heartfelt sigh escaped her lips. "But I must move, and very soon. I must get home. I have some things to do. And I have a date tonight."

"A date?" Hank repeated, jolting up, away from her. His eyes blazed into hers. "With whom?"

Laura could feel the tension contracting his muscles. A conciliatory smile curved her soft mouth. "With my family, Hank," she said in a soothing tone. "Once a month, Megan I have dinner with Brooke and Don, and then play bridge."

"Oh." The tension eased from his body. He left the bed and walked around the foot of it to pick up his clothes, supremely unconcerned about displaying his naked body before her. "Ah . . . did Megan question you about spending last night away from home?" he asked too casually.

"Not really," Laura moved her head from side to side, further tangling her already wildly disheveled hair. "All she asked was if it concerned a new client."

"And, of course, you could give her an unqualified yes in response."

Laura watched him warily, suddenly positive he was leading up to something she wasn't going to like. "Yes."

"Yes," he echoed, smiling faintly. "And what will you tell her next time, and the time after that?"

Feeling pressured, Laura sat up. Feeling insecure, she wrapped the sheet around her. "I don't know," she admitted. "I just don't know."

"Hmm." Hank rubbed one broad hand over his chest absently. Then he looked at her directly, his expression wry. "She's going to find out about us, you know."

Laura's eyes narrowed. "Not if I can help it." Her tone was adamant. "I won't have her hurt, Hank."

"I don't want her to be hurt, either." He slid his hand from his chest to the back of his neck. "But, dammit, Laura, she's bound to find out eventually and be hurt more by the deception, *our* deception." He drew a deep breath then said flatly, "I think you should tell her."

He was right; Laura knew he was right. But how did a mother tell her daughter that she was sleeping with the man the daughter believed herself in love with? "I can't!" Laura cried the answer aloud.

"I can."

Her head snapped up. "No! Hank, that's cruel! Megan's in love with you!"

"It's not cruel, it's honest," he retorted. "It's a helluva lot more honest than the two of us meeting in secret as if we're doing something to be ashamed of." Impatience roughened his voice. "In case you've forgotten, Megan is the child here, and you're the adult. Besides, I don't believe that Megan is in love with me. She barely knows me. If anything, she's got a bad case of misguided hero worship." His voice grew hard with insistence. "Laura, she has got to be told by one of us before she hears it from somebody else. There's no other way."

Feeling as though she'd been pushed to the edge of a choice between daughter and lover, Laura retaliated with attack. "Yes, there is another way," she said without thinking. "I can stop seeing you. Then there'll be nothing to tell."

Everything about Hank froze, except his eyes, which began to glitter with an inner heat. "Stop seeing me," he said much too softly. When the fire in his eyes reached flash point, he strode to her side. "Like hell!" he growled, flinging himself onto the bed and dragging her with him, beneath him.

Laura resisted, but it was an unequal contest; resisting Hank was like resisting every living cell in her body. His mouth was hot; his hands were restless; his intent was clear. Within minutes his need had aroused her. Eager for his possession, she invited it by curling her legs around his hips, and then cried aloud with his penetration deep into her body.

It was over quickly. Hank didn't spare her; Laura didn't want him to. Arched over her, his breathing sharp and harsh sounding, he stared into her passion-cloudy eyes. "Now," he said in a raspy voice. "Tell me that you can stop seeing me."

Laura closed her eyes in defeat. "I can't."

The sudden release of tension in his taut body, along with his roughly exhaled breath, betrayed the relief Hank felt. Lowering his head, he kissed her with tender concern. "I know. I understand how you feel," he murmured against her lips. "But in all fairness to Megan and to us, you must tell her."

"I will." Unmindful of the tears threatening to overflow her eyelids, Laura gazed into his softened eyes. "But, please, don't pressure me, Hank. Let me do it in my own way, at the proper time." She covered his mouth with her palm when he looked about to argue the point. "Please, allow me to do this my way. I can't just blurt it out. I must pick the time and place."

"And in the meantime, if we want to be together, it will have to be in secret," Hank said wearily.

Laura bit her lip but held firm to her position. "Yes."

Hank sighed with acceptance, but he maintained his stance of insistence. "All right, I won't pressure you. But I hope you find the right time and place soon, because I don't like playing the role of a sneak in the night."

"Mother! Hello. It's your bid."

Laura glanced up in confusion at the amused sound of Brooke's voice. "What?"

Brooke shot a "help me, save me" look at her husband and sister. "Are you half-asleep?" she chided. "I said it's your bid."

"Oh!" Avoiding the laughing eyes of the others, she concentrated on the cards in her hand. "Give me a moment, please."

"Maybe she is half-asleep," Megan observed, grinning when Laura looked up sharply. "You know she was out of town last night," she informed the other two at the card table. She wiggled her eyebrows suggestively. "She told me she was meeting a client, but maybe she had a rendezvous with some really scrumptious dude who kept her up most of the night."

"Megan!" Laura exclaimed, appalled because her teasing speculation was so close—too close—to the truth.

"Why, look at the color in her face!" Brooke laughed. "Mother! Confess. Is there some new exciting man in your life?"

Feeling trapped and guilty Laura raked her mind for a reply. Her son-in-law spared her the effort by springing to her rescue.

"C'mon, girls, cut your mother a break." He slanted a frowning glance from his wife to her sister. "If there is a man in Laura's life, it's certainly none of your business."

"Well I beg your pardon, Mr. Tobias!" Brooke said indignantly.

"Well, I beg to differ," Megan piped in. "She is *our* mother, you know."

"We have a right—" Brooke began.

"Bull," Don cut her off crudely. "You have the right to mind your own business. Your mother doesn't owe either one of you an explanation...about anything."

He sounded so much like Hank it was almost funny, but Laura wasn't amused, she was tired. Ignoring her daughters' arguments of protest, she placed her cards on the table, moved her chair back and said, "I'm going home."

"What?"

"You can't!"

"The game isn't finished!"

Laura smiled and responded to the group. "I said I'm going home. Yes, I can. And I don't care."

"Mother!" Brooke and Megan cried simultaneously.

"I'm outta here," Laura called from the front door, mimicking Megan's favorite expression. The last thing she heard as she shut the door behind her was the explosive sound of her son-in-law's laughter.

Laura's smile lasted all the way to the driveway, where she'd parked her car. How would Megan get home? she wondered as she inserted the key in the lock. Sighing, she pulled out the key and turned to go back for the girl. Don's soft call reached her before she took a step.

"Don't worry about Meg, Laura. I'll drive her home."

How well her family knew her, she mused, smiling wryly. Calling a soft, "Thank you," she got into the car and backed out of the driveway.

Laura's troubled thoughts kept her company all the way home. She had to tell Megan about Hank. She realized that now. Considering the speculation she'd caused by being away from home one night, Laura could easily imagine the conjecturing Brooke and Megan would indulge in if she continued to spend time away from home to be with Hank. And she had to be with Hank. He had proved that to her in the most graphic way possible.

But tell Megan? Laura shivered. She didn't know how to approach the subject. The girl believed herself to be in love and, regardless of what Hank said, Laura feared Megan would be more than hurt—she'd be devastated.

How did I get into this mess? she asked herself, automatically turning into her own driveway. *All I did was invite my daughter's employer to the house for the Easter holiday. Who would have thought that less than a week later I'd find myself in the throes of love?*

Laura's fingers gripped the steering wheel, as if to anchor herself to reality. Her mind was spinning.

Love? Who mentioned love? No one said a word about love. She couldn't be in love. Of course not! It wasn't possible to fall in love in less than a week. Was it? Besides, she didn't want to be in love. She didn't have time to be in love. Did she?

Love? What she felt was an illusion, not love. An illusion shaded by a midlife awakening of latent sensuality and pure old-fashioned lust. She wasn't in love with Hank. She couldn't be. Love was for young people like Megan and Brooke and Don. It wasn't for thirty-nine-year-old career-minded widows.

Love? Laura laughed. Then she choked on a sob. Oh, God. If Hank as much as suspected, she very likely wouldn't have to worry about telling Megan, because he'd be long gone.

"I don't want to be in love." Her voice sounded loud in the confines of the car.

But you are in love. Inside the confines of Laura's head, the immediate response sounded even louder.

Damn, she thought ironically. Growing up was as tough for mothers as it was for their children.

"Damn her!" Hank took a long swallow of beer from the icy can in an attempt to quench the rage boiling in his gut.

"To hell." The hard-voiced addendum came from the man seated opposite Hank at the chrome-and-glass kitchen table. "To the female of the species." He raised the can in his hand. "May they all rot in—"

"Luke!" Hank cut him off sharply. "Have you forgotten that your daughter's a female?"

Luke Branson frowned at his brother. "Yeah." His smile was wry. "But, you know, I don't think of Lyn as a female. I think of her as mine." Pain worked over his face, twisting it, and with a crash he slammed the beer can on the table. "Dammit, Hank! I've lost her. I've lost my baby!"

The ache that Hank felt for his younger brother went deep into his soul. He couldn't begin to imagine the pain involved in losing a child. But he could see the agony mirrored in Luke's face, could hear the pain in Luke's voice as he related his unsuccessful fight to gain legal custody of his daughter from his former wife. At a loss for appropriate words of commiseration, Hank shoved his chair back, circled the table and pulled his kid brother into his arms.

A sad smile feathered Hank's compressed mouth at the realization that his kid brother was hardly a kid anymore. At thirty-three, Luke was only three years his junior. In addition, his *kid* brother outstripped him by a good two and a half inches in height. And yet, at that moment, Luke was still his kid brother because, amazingly, he didn't give Hank a quick hug then move away in adult embarrassment.

Luke clung to Hank like a lost child. And like a lost child, Luke sobbed—for his own lost child.

Blinking against the sting of hot moisture filling his eyes, Hank held his brother and felt a sympathetic resentment for women surge through his mind and body.

A woman had brought Luke to this state of hate and despair; a woman greedy for the material possessions another, wealthier man could give her. And that woman, the woman Luke had loved above all others, had not only betrayed Luke with her body, she had taken his child from him.

Rage consumed Hank as he stood, clasping his brother close to his own comforting strength. And it was not only rage at the perfidious woman who had grabbed the main chance in the form of a wealthy Englishman, escaping to England, where courts inclined to rule in favor of one of their own. Hank's rage included the woman who had run from him with his best friend . . . and all women in general.

Laura.

Thinking her name brought her image, and Hank winced. Was Laura capable of the kind of treachery he and Luke had suffered at the hands of two members of her sex?

Not Laura. Hank rejected the idea at once. She was too sincere, too forthright, too honest.

Sincere. Forthright. Honest. And yet he had had to force the issue by insisting Laura end the secrecy of their affair by telling her daughter about their relationship.

Hank didn't like the suspicious trend of his thoughts and felt a wave of relief when Luke interrupted the reverie by disengaging himself from his arms.

"Sorry about that, Hank," he apologized, scraping his hands over the wet tracks on his gaunt face. "I appreciate the support." Luke's strong features settled into an unrevealing mask. "It won't happen again." His smile was bitter and unyielding. "No woman will ever again get the opportunity to rip me apart with her dainty manicured claws." His lips twisted. "In the future, if anyone's going to be used, it sure as hell won't be me. Depend on it."

Hank believed him; it was impossible not to believe him. Ruthless determination was indelibly stamped on his face and blazed like icy fire from his dark eyes. Hank suddenly felt sorry for any woman, good, bad, or indifferent, who happened to have the misfortune to find herself within Luke's sphere of influence. For, in all honesty, his brother was as handsome as the devil and, from now on, *devil* was the operative word.

In that instant Hank knew he didn't want Luke to meet Laura. He didn't want Luke within shouting distance of Laura. She was too feminine, too soft. And, considering the vow he'd just made, Luke would take one look, have her measure and then destroy her.

And then I'd have to destroy him.

The spontaneous thought stunned Hank. Why had he had such a ridiculous thought? Where had it sprung from? Luke was his brother!

Laura was his love.

Hank was staggered by the solid assurance contained in the abrupt thought. His love? Laura? No! He enjoyed Laura. He had fun with Laura. He *made* love with Laura. But, damned if he was *in* love with Laura! He'd been in love before. And he had never considered himself a slow learner. Being in love tore the guts out of a man and made him weak. Not being in love kept a man strong. Weren't he and Luke perfect examples?

They were and . . .

"How about some pizza or something, Hank?" Luke asked, interrupting Hank's mental flow of denial. "This excess of emotion has left me hungry. You want to go out and get something to eat?"

Eat. Hank recalled cold chicken nuggets and tepid wine. At the time, he'd considered the fast food little less than ambrosia. Love? Shrugging, he pushed the notion to the depths of his consciousness.

"Sure, why not?" he replied, striding beside Luke to the door.

Love. Love was for teenagers and suckers.

Wasn't it?

The question teased Hank's tired mind long after he and Luke had returned to the apartment and said good-night. He had reasons, excellent reasons, to be wary of an emotional attachment to any woman. But, then, Laura wasn't just any woman. Laura was... Hank writhed in the agony of defining what Laura was to him. She was a part of him now. A part of his flesh, a part of his mind, a part of his soul.

But, dammit! He didn't want to love any woman!

Nine

Feeling different and oddly changed by the realization that she was in love with Hank, Laura intuitively felt the change in him the minute he entered the model house on Monday afternoon. He was not cold, but slightly reserved; not exactly rude, but impatient and abrupt.

She was working in the dining room when he came in. Made wary by his austere expression, Laura gave him a tentative smile. Hank didn't smile back or waste time with the formality of a civil greeting.

"Did you talk to Megan?" he asked rather imperiously.

Laura didn't appreciate his tone or his manner; she didn't appreciate being pressured, either. Her smile reflected the chill permeating her being. "Hello to you, too," she said, raising her chin a notch. He wasn't impressed or intimidated.

"Did you tell her?" Hank snapped.

"No!" Laura snapped back.

"No?" His eyes narrowed as he slowly walked to her. Standing over her, Hank planted his hands on his hips and leveled a drilling stare at her. "Why not?" he demanded. "You told me you would."

Two long nights spent in fruitless speculation and self-examination instead of peaceful slumber suddenly caught up with Laura. Her patience began to fray round the edges. She might have been foolish enough to fall in love with the man, but she certainly wasn't so besotted she'd allow him to dictate to her. She was even older than him! Laura reminded herself, meeting his famous glare with cool directness.

"What I said—exactly—was that I would pick the proper time and place to talk to Megan," she replied distinctly.

A muscle rippled along Hank's clenched jawline. "You had all weekend to find the proper time and place," he said tightly. "You had ample opportunity to speak to her."

"All weekend!" Laura exploded. "I had Saturday evening and yesterday!" She paused to draw in a calming breath. "And, if you recall, I told you Megan and I had arrangements made to spend Saturday evening with Brooke and Don." She refrained from offering the information of how early she left her daughter's home, or why. "And as for yesterday," she went on, "I saw Megan for a total of two hours, one in the morning before she left the house to meet some friends, and the other before she went to bed after she returned." She reflected his belligerent stance by placing her much smaller hands on her slender hips. "That is hardly what I'd call ample opportunity," she finished heatedly, letting her anger show.

"So, until the proper time and place occurs, we continue playing the role-reversal game," Hank growled. "Correct me if I'm wrong, but doesn't this usually work the other way around? I mean, I thought it was the kid who had clandestine meetings with a lover, not the parent."

Out of patience with him—possibly because he was right—Laura spun away to pace the width of the room. "Hank, please, try to see this from my position," she implored him. "You know the circumstances."

"I know this whole situation is crazy!" he retorted. "I'm thirty-six, you're thirty-nine, and we're forced to sneak around to be together, like teenagers, meeting secretly, hiding out, and all because a nineteen-year-old thinks she's in love!"

"That nineteen-year-old is my daughter, Hank." Laura's tone held a hint of warning; he had aroused the protective maternal instinct in her.

He stared at her in frustration for a long moment, then he turned and strode to the archway in the foyer. "All right, I'll play the stupid game a little longer." He paused in the archway to glance back at her. "But will you do me a favor?"

"If I can," Laura agreed at once, relieved that the confrontation appeared to be over. "What is it?"

He ran a bleak glance over the barren room. "See if you can hurry up the decorating process in here," he replied. "If we have to hide out, let's at least do it in relative comfort."

"I'll see what I can do," she promised.

When it came to decorating, even hasty decorating, Laura did very well. By the end of that week the house was beginning to look like a home—in truth, it looked like Hank's home. For even though Laura was forced to settle for pieces of furniture that were readily available instead of waiting for the things she had originally decided upon that had to be specially ordered, her alternate choices were all made with Hank in mind.

Unfortunately, when it came to maintaining her equilibrium in a personal relationship of the male/female, one-on-one variety, Laura was a better decorator than maintainer.

She was in love, and growing more so with each passing day. But, rather than making her euphoric with happiness, the emotion filled her with questions and doubts.

Was she acting wisely by becoming deeply involved with a man at this point in her life? That was the primary question. There were numerous other questions along the same line that persisted in tormenting her at odd moments of the day and night. Questions like, was she too settled in her career and role of mother to change her life-style? And, wasn't she a bit past the age of the grand passion? And, what would she do when the affair, admittedly very hot, began to cool?

Her doubts mainly concerned Hank. How did he feel, truly feel, about her? He had said he thought she was wonderful, but he had never uttered a word about commitment. He was acting strained and reserved already. Was his behavior an early indication of waning interest?

The questions and doubts buzzed inside her mind, constant companions to her every unrelated thought. In consequence, Laura's demeanor was less open, more guarded when she was alone with him.

The uncertainty froze her tongue whenever she as much as thought about talking to Megan. So she kept putting it off, telling herself the time wasn't quite right.

That week slipped into another, and then another, during which Laura and Hank met at the house every second or third day. The house was warm and welcoming. Their lovemaking was hot and satisfying. Their relationship appeared to be growing more tenuous with each successive meeting. They began to argue, always over unimportant things, like food and clothes and, on one stormy night, the weather, of all things.

By the first week of May, Laura was beginning to feel as though she were struggling to stay afloat in a bog of quicksand, and she was getting pretty tired of the sensation.

Hank was in a state of inner conflict. While a part of him, the major part of him, urged him to declare his love for Laura and end the constraint between them, a tiny portion of him advised restraint.

Having Luke around to remind him of the deceptive capabilities of women did little to ease Hank's dilemma. Though Luke never mentioned the subject of women after his outburst on the night of his arrival, his presence was a constant reminder of how it felt to be used then discarded by a woman.

Hank's rage had been aroused while he clasped his brother in his arms, and had spilled out onto Laura the following Monday. Since then, it had subsided to a simmering anger, close to the surface, ready to erupt at the slightest provocation.

And Laura still had not managed to find the proper time to talk to Megan. Her reluctance to do so fed the anger inside Hank. His anger was tainting their relationship. Hank knew it and reacted by becoming even more angry and mistrustful.

The situation couldn't endure; something, or someone, had to give. Laura innocently set the match to the short fuse. After weeks of sustained tension, the resultant explosion was inevitable.

It was midafternoon when Laura arrived at the house. The weather had turned unusually hot, and she was dressed accordingly in a sleeveless summer blouse, a lightweight straight skirt and next-to-nothing sandals that drew the eye to her slender legs and slim feet. Her hair swirled free around her shoulders and gleamed in the bright sunlight when she moved. Large gold hoop earrings glittered against her dark hair, lending an interesting combination of both the exotic and the casual to her appearance.

That morning, Laura had dressed with the clear intention of pleasing Hank. She had deliberately arrived at the house early to prepare dinner for him. Tired of the constant strain and take-out meals, she was hoping that a relaxing dinner followed by some candid conversation would be a start in the right direction toward easing the difficulties between them.

After pausing to admire the end result of her efforts in the foyer and living room, Laura headed toward the kitchen. She took one step into the dining room and came to a staggering halt, gasping in shock at the sight of wanton destruction that met her horrified eyes.

The sliding-glass patio doors had been shattered. The expensive carpet was littered with splintered glass, dark potting soil and broken shards of a large potted fern that had stood sentinel inside the doors and two large rocks that had obviously been hurled through the glass.

Feeling almost personally violated, Laura stared in disbelief at the devastation, one hand clamped to her mouth. Who? Why? she thought, shaking her head slowly. Then she thought of Hank! Spinning around, she ran from the house. She had to find Hank!

Laura knew a crew of men were tiling a roof on the house located to the north of the model home. She saw Hank as she approached the property; she could hardly miss him. He was working beside another man on the roof, laying tile, stripped to the waist. She walked to within shouting distance of him, ignoring the wolf whistles and catcalls from the men working in the immediate area. Hearing the ruckus, Hank stood up to investigate before she had a chance to call out. She saw his eyes widen on sight of her and heard the anger in his voice when he barked a sharp order to his men.

"Knock it off, you clowns!" He stood tall at the very edge of the roof, causing her to fear for his safety. "What is it, Laura?" His voice was softer, but his anger was still apparent. Laura was too upset to notice.

"Hank!" she cried. "I must talk to you. Somebody broke into the house!"

"God!" His curse was carried to her by the breeze. "Stay there. I'm coming down." He strode along the edge of the roof to an access ladder and descended it with the agility of a veteran logger. Laura had barely resumed breathing when he walked up to her, caught her by the arm and steered her into his dust-coated van.

"What happened?" he demanded, firing the engine. The van shot away from the building site before she could get out a word.

"Somebody threw two large rocks through the patio doors," Laura explained, hanging on to her seat for dear life. "The glass was shattered." She paused as he brought the van to a jarring stop at the house. "As was the clay pot sitting inside. The dining room's a mess."

"Anything else broken or missing?" Hank asked, striding into the house.

"I didn't wait to investigate," Laura panted, running to keep up with him. "I came straight to you."

"Good." Hank stopped dead in the dining room archway. "Damn it," he swore, biting out each word separately. "What kind of idiot would do this?" He studied the debris on the floor, then turned so suddenly he nearly plowed into her. "You stay here," he ordered tersely. "I'm going to check out the rest of the place."

Getting a brush and dustpan from the laundry room, Laura began to clean up the mess. She was hunched down, brushing dirt and glass into the pan when Hank returned to the room.

"What in hell are you doing?" He exploded, charging across the room.

"I'm cleaning up," Laura replied, reaching for a jagged piece of glass.

"Leave it," he ordered sharply, snatching the glass from her hand and dropping it back onto the floor. "I'll send a man in to do it tomorrow morning." Grasping her arms, he pulled her up before him. "And what the hell are you trying to prove by parading around in front of my men looking like that?" he snarled in an angry-sounding whisper.

"What?" Laura looked at him in blank astonishment.

"You need proof that you're attractive to men?" he asked in a dangerous tone of voice. "I'll give you all the proof you need." Dropping one arm to the back of her thighs, he swung her off the floor and into his arms.

"Hank!" Laura cried in protest as he carried her from the room and up the stairs.

The suddenness of his action made her senses spin. It seemed that one moment she was kneeling down in the dining room, and moments later she was flat on her back on the large bed in the master suite, flinching at the resounding bang of the door slamming shut.

"Hank! What are you doing?" Laura cried.

Hank chided her with a sardonic smile. "You want a detailed play-by-play of the game plan?" he drawled, putting his hands to work on his belt buckle.

Laura felt somewhat scared and somewhat thrilled and altogether confused. What had she done to make him so angry? And Hank *was* angry—furiously angry. It was written on his taut features, glittering in his eyes. But why? And why had he made that insulting remark about her parading around in front of his men? She had never paraded around in front of any man...except him! Perplexed, Laura lay still, puzzling over his strange incomprehensible behavior.

"Hank..." Her voice failed when he turned his back to her to sit on the end of the bed to remove his boots. When it returned it was edged with impatience. "I don't understand!"

As he stood up, Hank fixed a calculating stare on her and coolly stepped out of his tan work pants and kicked them aside. "Laura..." he said, mocking her exasperated tone and raking her body with a cool glance. "Only one of us is getting undressed here." He hooked his thumbs in the elastic band of his briefs and slid them down over his taut flanks. He arched his dark brows as he started toward her. "Or were you hoping I'd help you?"

Prone on the bed, Laura swallowed dryly as she watched him approach and wondered how it was possible for a man to look threatening and appealing at one and the same time. His tan skin was slick with the sweat he'd produced working on the roof in the hot sun. He smelled of fresh air and sunshine and musky aroused male. Wetting her parched lips, she began inching backwards away from him. "I...I don't understand what you're doing."

"Sure you do." Hank's smile sent shivers skipping along her rigid spine. His glittering eyes monitored her awkward attempt to back away. "You should've loosened your skirt," he observed dryly, closing in on the bed, and her. "By now, you'd have wiggled halfway out of it."

Laura grew still and placed her palms flat on the mattress on either side of her. "If you're trying out a new method of sensual teasing, I don't like it," she said in what sounded like an excited gasp to her own ears. But it was true; she didn't like it. And yet she found it terribly arousing.

Hank correctly read the conflict in her voice and the anticipation sparkling in her eyes. He laughed as he bent over her. "I'm getting impatient." His fingers made swift expert work of the button and zipper closings at the side of her skirt. "Let me help you." With one smooth long sweep, he whisked her skirt, panty hose and satin panties over her hips and down her legs. He flipped her sandals across the room and tossed her clothing after them.

"Hank! Stop it!" Laura cried, more aroused than scared. "Enough is enough, and I've—"

His mouth swallowed her protest; his body blanketed hers. Lying full length on her, Hank kissed her senseless. By the time he lifted his mouth from hers, Laura was moaning low in her throat and urging him into the cradle of her thighs by tugging on his taut buttocks with her restless hands.

Hank resisted her efforts, holding his body a brief tantalizing distance from hers. "Did I hear you say you had had enough?" he taunted. "Would you like me to stop?"

"No!" Laura's eyes blazed into his, silently telling him that if she didn't need him so desperately at that moment she'd happily slap him.

He smiled in understanding of her visually relayed message and continued to torment her. "Would you like me to proceed?'' Swaying gently, he brushed his body against hers.

"Yes!"

"Like this?'' He arched into her, then immediately withdrew.

"Yes!'' Laura stared at him in bewilderment. What was he doing? And why was he doing it?

"Do you want me, Laura?'' Bending low, Hank tortured the crest of one breast with his flicking tongue. "Only me?'' His hoarse voice seemed to echo in the valley of her breast.

"Yes.'' Strangely, Laura was no longer afraid of the new hard-edged side of himself that he was revealing to her. She was confused by the suddenness of it, the reason for it. "Hank, please, I don't under—'' she began again when he lifted his head to pin her with his hot amber eyes.

"Say it!'' His voice was soft but steely with insistence.

"I want you.'' She had no difficulty saying the words he was intent on hearing, because they were absolutely true. "I want you!'' she repeated more strongly. "Only you.''

"You're mine, Laura. Mine. Remember it.'' The harshness of his tone was tempered by the betraying tremor that shivered through his long body.

At that instant Laura would have given him more than confirmation of her physical need of him; she'd have given him a fervent confession of her love for him. But at that instant, Hank surged into her with more strength and power than he had ever before shown her.

In a tiny lucid corner of Laura's mind, she thought vaguely that it was as if Hank were making a declaration of territorial rights with his powerful possession of her. But then the thought was gone, swept from her mind by the pleasure he was giving to her and demanding from her.

It would be weeks later that Laura would realize that she had conceived Hank's child at the culmination of their passionate lovemaking. While it was happening, she didn't feel capable of conceiving a coherent thought, never mind a child.

When it was over, Hank lay beside her, his deep breaths sounding harsh and loud in the quiet room. Exhausted, yet ultimately fulfilled, Laura forced her eyes open when he turned his head on the pillow to stare at her.

"Did I hurt you?" His features were drawn, his lips were compressed, his beautiful eyes were shadowed. There was an unnatural stillness about him, and the stoic look of a brave man waiting for the ax to fall on his neck.

Longing to erase that odd haunted look from his face, she smiled and murmured, "No, Hank, you didn't hurt me."

He didn't return her smile. His expression didn't alter by as much as a flicker. "Did I frighten you?"

"Frighten me?" she repeated, frowning. Laura raised herself up on one elbow to face him squarely. "No, Hank, you didn't hurt me and you didn't frighten me. Why? Were you trying to?"

"No," he said, turning away to roll off the bed. "I was just wondering."

He was lying to her. Laura knew he'd lied as surely as she suddenly knew that for some unfathomable reason, Hank had actually wanted to punish her. The knowledge hurt her, and the pain went deep. Hank had wanted to hurt her, he had wanted to frighten her, and he lied to her by denying both.

Her eyes concealed by her lowered lashes, Laura watched Hank averting his gaze from the bed, and her, while collecting his clothes and striding into the bathroom.

The intuitive feeling she'd had weeks ago settled into a certainty. He was not the same man she had shared cold chicken and laughter with a few short weeks ago. Almost overnight something had occurred that had changed Hank from the warm teasing laughing lover he'd been before, into a cool withdrawn stranger who felt it necessary to frighten and hurt her to wring an admission of her desire for him from her.

Laura couldn't imagine what could have occurred to bring about such a drastic change in Hank and in such a short amount of time. All she knew was that it had altered and strained their relationship to the limits of her endurance.

Suddenly all her questions and doubts of the previous weeks were resolved. Even loving Hank as deeply as she did, Laura knew she couldn't continue to function in an atmosphere of tension and constraint.

Dragging her depleted depressed body from the bed, Laura smoothed the spread, picked up her clothes and quietly left the room to dress in another bathroom.

"You're a stupid fool, Branson."

Hank's muttered accusation was drowned in the

water drumming against the shower walls and floor. The gushing cadence kept time with the beat inside his skull. His head hurt, but then, an attack of conscience always had that effect on him. Deciding he'd punished himself long enough by standing directly in the line of fire of the pounding spray, Hank shut off the taps and stepped out of the cubicle.

What was she doing? Crying? The speculative thought raised goose bumps on his flesh unrelated to the chilling water that had showered down his body. If she was crying, he was at fault. Jolting around, Hank grabbed a crimson towel from a glass rod. Hell, he was at fault if she wasn't crying!

Laura.

Her name was a groan deep in Hank's soul. The silent groan was manifest aloud as a curse on his tight lips. He had hurt her, the woman who had given him more pleasure in a multitude of ways than he had ever dared hope of experiencing in an entire lifetime. And he had hurt her. Deliberately.

Cursing under his breath, Hank dried the moisture from his body then flung the towel to the floor. Dammit! He had had reasons for his actions! Yeah, all of them bad. Exhaling a tired sigh, he picked up the towel and draped it over the rod. As he shrugged into his clothes, his jaw squared with purpose. He owed her an apology. Hell, he owed her a lot more than that. But, for now, he'd work on the apology.

After he was dressed, Hank pulled open the door and strode into the bedroom. Laura was gone. The bed had been tidied. Everything was tidy. And Laura was gone. A sick gut feeling told him that she was not only gone from the bedroom, but from the house and the subdivision. He didn't even go to the window to see if her car was no longer parked outside. He knew it wasn't. Crossing the room, he sank onto the end of the bed.

How had he managed to get himself into this situation to begin with? Hank asked himself, absently smoothing his hand over the blatantly sensual spread.

Rage. He had reacted to years of accumulated rage. Rage for what one woman had once done to him. Rage for what another woman had done to his brother. But, mostly, rage driven by fear for what the most important woman could do to him now.

Hank faced his unpalatable thoughts, then took them one step further. Fueled by jealousy, his rage had finally slipped his control that afternoon when he'd heard the unmistakable effect of Laura's appearance on his men. When he'd glanced around at her from his perch on the roof, she had looked stunningly beautiful, achingly desirable, all woman.

At that moment, needing her desperately and afraid of that need, he had set out to punish Laura for making him feel again, love again. But it had been the fear of losing her that had driven him to force her to admit her need for him.

And what had his imposing macho performance gotten him? Hank asked himself, pushing his tired body off the bed. He walked to the door and turned to look back into the room she had so obviously decorated for him.

The bed was empty. The room was empty. He was empty.

Laura was gone.

Ten

Laura viewed the Memorial Day weekend with less than enthusiasm. It was hot. It was sticky. She was pregnant.

Since the warm weather was a usual annual occurrence, it really didn't bother Laura. Being pregnant did; that phenomenon hadn't occurred to her for twenty years. She had long since forgotten what morning sickness felt like. Now she was reminded every morning with tiresome regularity.

Late Friday afternoon, Laura sat slumped in her desk chair, staring into middle distance. She knew she should call it a day and go home. A list of things still to be done in preparation for her traditional first-of-the-season holiday cookouts lay before her on the desk top. The list seemed endless. The prospect was daunting. Laura was tired.

"Are you all right?"

Laura glanced up with an automatic smile at the concerned note in Ginnie's voice. "I'm fine," she lied easily, a talent developed by necessity during the previous three weeks, since every member of her family except Heather had asked her that same question at least once.

Ginnie's flame-shaded eyebrows drew together. "You don't look fine to me. In fact, you look exhausted."

Laura moved her shoulders in a listless shrug. "It's been pretty busy around here the past few weeks."

"You mean *you've* been busy," Ginnie corrected her wryly. "You've taken on the work load of three people."

"Might as well grab it while it's there," Laura said, excusing her frantic activity evasively.

"Hmm-hmm." Ginnie's murmur held a skeptical intonation. "Whatever happened to that gorgeous hunk of male contractor who insisted you personally decorate the model house in his subdivision?" Her bland expression was belied by the interest sparkling her jewel-green eyes.

This time, Laura concentrated on executing a careless shrug. "Nothing happened to him," she replied with hard-fought-for insouciance. "I completed the commission ahead of schedule, he sent a check, along with a generous bonus," she explained smoothly, not adding the additional information that she had returned the bonus check—in two equal-size halves.

"Strange," Ginnie murmured.

"That he sent a check?"

The redhead's smile was feline. "No," she purred. "Strange because he hasn't been in evidence since then. I would have sworn he was interested in you...as in man-woman interested."

"It isn't at all strange," Laura disagreed, fighting for all she was worth to maintain her composure. "My understanding is that Hank Branson is wary of women because of a rather bad relationship some years ago." The results of which *she* had been punished for, Laura thought, standing abruptly. The conversation was making her feel nauseated; it was time to go home. "Let's pack it in for the weekend," she said briskly, pulling the bottom desk drawer open to retrieve her purse. "Everything here will wait until Tuesday."

"Excellent suggestion," Ginnie drawled, pushing her chair away from her desk. "Why didn't I think of that?"

Within minutes Laura was locking the showroom door. "Come anytime on Monday," she said, smiling at the younger woman. As a rule, Ginnie spent every holiday with her family. But, since her family were all gathering somewhere in the Midwest for a combined reunion and Memorial Day celebration, Ginnie had decided to forego the traveling and give it a miss. When Laura heard she'd be alone on the holiday, she had immediately invited Ginnie to her cookout; Ginnie had immediately accepted.

"Breakfast?" Ginnie grinned.

"Anytime after lunch," Laura qualified with a smile as she started toward her car. She was about to slip behind the wheel when the younger woman called to her.

"Can I bring something?"

"Just your charming self," Laura replied, waving a goodbye as she drove away.

Laura's smile collapsed the instant she was out of Ginnie's sight. A long sigh escaped her lips. She felt tired, so very tired. And though she would have liked to believe her excessive weariness was caused by her condition, she knew, deep down inside, that the early symptoms of pregnancy were only partly to blame.

She was pining for Hank. Laura felt the sting of tears in her eyes as an image of him flashed into her mind. The three weeks that had passed since she'd walked out of his bedroom, his house and his life, were the longest weeks she had ever lived through.

Hank had called her once, later that same night. Laura could still hear him, the sound of remorse in his voice as he asked her to forgive him and the overshadowing of insistence when he asked her to meet him at the house the next day. She could still hear the sound of her own voice, the softness when she accepted his apology, the sadness when she told him it was over.

At the time Laura was positive she had made the right decision, the only possible decision she could make. She had questioned the wisdom of her decision every waking and sleeping minute since then.

When she first became suspicious about her condition, Laura had felt giddy with joy. She was pregnant! She was going to have Hank's child! She couldn't wait for the natural progression of time to confirm her suspicions. She had to know, immediately, if not sooner! The test results were as close to immediate as Laura could get. A confusion of thoughts raced through her mind as she replaced the telephone receiver after hearing her physician confirm her suspicions.

A baby! She was thirty-nine years old, and she was going to have a baby! No, she wasn't going to have *a* baby. She was going to have *Hank's* baby!

Euphoric, Laura had reached for the phone again. She couldn't wait to tell him. Hank had never been married. He had never had a child. He'd be ecstatic. He'd be delirious! He'd be... At that point, Laura's euphoric bubble burst. In the real world, she knew exactly what Hank would be. He'd be convinced that he had been used by yet another woman. But, being Hank, he would insist they marry at once.

Unmindful of the tears running down her face, Laura drove adroitly through the heavy start-of-the-holiday traffic and relived the emotional conflict she'd suffered during the past couple of days.

Her initial reaction to the realization that Hank would in all probability insist on marriage was a determination not to tell him about the baby. It was her baby, she'd thought irrationally. It was in her body. Who needed him? She did, of course, but that was beside the point. But Hank had a right to know, she'd chided herself. His rights were equal to hers where the child was concerned.

But she didn't want to marry Hank. Well, she did, but not by entrapment. And Laura was certain Hank would consider it an entrapment. And, in the final analysis, the absolutely last thing Laura wanted was to call or go to Hank like a teenager in *trouble*!

She wasn't in trouble; she could well afford to raise a child by herself; she had already raised two children by herself. And she wasn't a teenager. She was a mature thirty-nine-year-old woman. She was a career woman. And thirty-nine-year-old career women did not *have* to get married!

But Hank had a right to know. Laura realized she would have to tell him, and soon. She would tell him after the holiday.

Laura parked her car in the garage, then wiped the tears from her face with an impatient swipe of her hand. She blew her nose, then concealed the telltale red splotches with repeated dabs of her compact puff.

Megan might be home, and Megan didn't usually miss much.

A wry smile played at the corners of Laura's mouth as she got out of the car. To her admittedly emotional way of thinking, the only beneficial result of her breakup with Hank had been the removal of the weight from Laura of telling Megan about their affair.

"She's not worth it."

Hank jolted around to frown at Luke. "Who's not worth what?" he asked quietly.

Luke's long, too thin body was sprawled in lazy abandon on a patio lounge chair. "Whoever it is that you've been brooding about for nearly a month." A cynical smile twisted his otherwise attractive mouth. "There isn't a woman living worth five minutes of any man's brooding time, let alone a month."

It hadn't been a month; it had been exactly three weeks. Hank knew; he'd kept meticulous count of the days and berated himself for a fool every minute of every one of them.

Laura.

Swallowing against a sudden thickness in his throat, Hank turned away from the sardonic expression on his brother's gaunt face to stare sightlessly at the newly planted trees Laura had ordered weeks ago from the nursery.

It hurt just to think about her, and yet Hank had given up his apartment in town to move into the house she had decorated for him. Moving into the house had been a deliberate act for Hank. He had wanted to be there, needed to be there, because he felt close to Laura while in the house.

Hank wasn't thirsty, but he raised his beer can to his mouth just to give his hand something to do. In retrospect, it seemed that everything he did since she'd walked away from the house, from him, had been done to give him something to do.

The days were long. The nights were longer. He hurt like hell.

"Don't want to talk about it, huh?" Luke jackknifed from the lounge chair with surprising agility.

"With you?" Hank slanted a wry look at the man as he strolled to his side.

Luke tilted his can in a casual salute. "Right. I'm not exactly what anyone would call the sympathetic type when it comes to women."

"Not exactly!" Hank choked on his beer. "On the topic of women, you're about as sympathetic as a cornered rattler."

Luke shrugged with easy acceptance of the insult. "Once burned, and all that." His dark eyes settled on his brother. "You've experienced the heat of the fire, Hank," Luke reminded him. "The searing pain isn't worth the momentary warmth."

Hank had spent three incredibly long weeks contemplating the theory his brother espoused. He'd reached his own conclusion. "In fear of being burned, a man can get damned cold."

Luke stared at him long and hard, then shook his head in despair. "You're hell-bent on plunging back into the flame, aren't you?" he said.

"I love her, Luke." It was the first time Hank had said the words aloud. Deciding he liked the sound of them, he repeated the declaration. "I love her."

"Does she love you?"

"I thought so. I think so. There was a . . . misunderstanding." Hank sighed. "But, God, I hope so."

"What are you going to do about it?"

Hank had given that a great deal of thought. The idea of phoning Laura was unsatisfactory—besides, he'd tried that and it hadn't helped. He needed to see her. Talk to her. He had been toying with an idea . . . On a hunch, Hank decided to give it a try. "Do?" he finally replied. "Why, I'm going to have a long talk with a nineteen-year-old girl."

In crisp white tennis shorts, a sleeveless bright orange slipover top and flat sandals, Laura looked closer to twenty-nine than thirty-nine. Smiling as she wove through the crowd of guests, she didn't look tired or pregnant. Her appearance and her zest were a sham—she felt beat.

People were everywhere—in the house, on the small patio, in the yard, in the driveway and in the garage . . . mostly in the garage, since that was where the bar was set up.

She was on her way from the kitchen to the long trestle tables under the trees at the base of the yard when Megan materialized beside her.

"Mother, I hope you don't mind, but I invited two more guests to join the party."

"What's two more in this crush?" Laura laughed, and stifled a tired sigh.

"Thanks, Mom." Megan gave her a quick surprising kiss on the cheek. "You won't regret it." Whirling away, she headed for a group of her friends on the patio.

Regret it? Laura frowned, then chuckled softly. She probably wouldn't even notice the new arrivals.

Shrugging, she continued on to the tables, where Brooke and Ginnie were helping Ruth lay out the food.

"Are you sure you have enough here to eat?" Ginnie asked dryly, indicating the laden tables with a sweep of her arm.

"You're new to this," Ruth observed sagely. "Wait till the horde descends. You'll see how fast the food disappears."

"Yeah," Brooke interjected. "We may even have to send out for pizza later."

Smiling serenely, Laura listened to their banter while rearranging several platters on a table. A moment later she very nearly dropped a relish plate when she heard her daughter's soft exclamation.

"Oh, yummy! Mother, you didn't tell me you'd invited Hank Branson!"

Hank? For a long second, Laura couldn't breathe or think or speak. Megan! The name jumped into her mind when her brain began functioning again. "I . . . ah, didn't," she finally managed to say. "Your sister did." *And I just might throttle her,* she thought wildly.

"Who is that man with Mr. Branson?" Ginnie asked in an extremely interested purr. "He's a bit thin, but, oh my, he is a dark and handsome devil."

Man? Up until that instant, Laura hadn't even noticed the man walking towards them at Hank's side. She spared a brief glance for him but swiftly returned her hungry gaze to Hank. He looked tan and fit and wonderful, and she hated him for it when she felt so miserable.

"Ms. Miller. Ms. Devlon. Brooke." Hank smiled and nodded to the three women before turning his attention to his hostess. "Laura," he murmured, star-

ing straight into her eyes. "Thank you for inviting us."
He released his visual hold on her on his last word.
"I'd like you to meet my brother," he said, turning to
the other man, "Luke Branson."

Laura saw the man's lips move, heard his words of
greeting, but felt...only Hank. She felt him all the way
to the heart of the child growing inside her body. She
felt him so strongly, so deeply, she missed the words
he spoke to her after the introductions were over.

"I beg your pardon?"

Hank's eyes narrowed. "I asked if you could spare
me a moment for a private conversation," he said
tightly.

Laura's heart leaped, then immediately plum-
meted. "A private conversation?" She glanced around
at the mob of people closing in on the tables. "Here?"

"Of course not!" Hank took a deep breath, then
went on more calmly. "If you'll follow me?" He held
out his hand.

Laura's palm itched with the need to touch his. "I
can't." She glanced around again. "I have guests to
see to."

"Nonsense!" Ruth snorted. "You go along. I can
handle the food and the hungry horde."

"I'll help Ruth, Mother," Brooke offered. "Take
a break—you've certainly earned it."

"And I'll be happy to help Mr. Branson get acquainted with everyone," Ginnie volunteered, coura-
geously meeting Luke's cynical smile.

Well, in that case... Laura placed her hand in
Hank's. Striking out ahead of her, he ran interfer-
ence for her through the converging guests. As they
skirted the patio, Laura shot a frantic look at Megan
and exhaled a big breath of relief when the girl grinned
and sent her the thumbs-up signal.

Since the guests had gravitated toward the food, the driveway was empty, which made their passage a lot faster. Laura was gasping for breath by the time they reached his car, parked on the street in the next block.

"Did you happen to notice Megan as we made our escape?" Hank asked after they were settled in the car.

"Yes," Laura panted. "Do you know what she was trying to tell me?"

"That she approves," Hank said uninformatively. He started the engine and set the car in motion—fast motion.

"Approves of what?" Laura asked, checking her seat belt to make sure it was secure.

"Of us being together."

Laura stared at him in amazement. "But how did she know?"

Hank shot a grin at her. "I told her."

"You didn't hurt her?" she demanded fiercely.

"Did she look hurt?"

Laura calmed down a little. "No, but—"

"There are no 'buts,' Laura." Hank shook his head as if to say, who can understand young people? "She was amazed that you still thought she was in love with me." His smile was wry. "She told me she got over that case of hero worship when I barked an order at her the week after Easter."

Laura laughed. She really should have known. Why hadn't she? The thought startled the laughter from her; her mouth curved into a rueful smile. In retrospect, Laura realized that all the signs were there, indicating another one of Megan's mercurial mind changes. She had been spending a lot of time out of the house with friends. And, on reflection, Laura suddenly recalled that Megan's conversation lately had been liberally peppered with the name of one particular young man...even though the actual name eluded Laura at the moment. Was it Jason? Judson? Justin? She mentally shrugged. No matter, she'd find out soon enough; she'd make a point of finding out.

But, to Laura, comprehending her own laxity in regard to her daughter's emotional state was of far greater importance at the moment than the given name of a young man.

Comprehension came with such stunning swiftness, Laura blinked. She was in love, so very much in love with Hank, that she had been blind to everything and everybody around her, even to thoughts of her family.

For one flashing instant, Laura felt smothered by guilt and inadequacy. Then her common sense took command and squashed the unearned feelings. Her daughters were adults, no longer requiring or requesting her constant guidance. She had a right to her own life, her own love. If, indeed, he was her love.

Laura stole a glance at Hank's profile and was forced to swallow against the sudden tightness in her throat. He had said Megan approve of them being together. Did that mean he intended them to be together? Optimism rose inside her, optimism and expectation and a yearning so strong if stole her breath. She loved him so, needed him so, it was almost scary.

Positive that Hank would read her desire in her eyes if he happened to shift his gaze from the road to her, Laura turned away to look out the side window. The first sight that registered was a familiar landmark they were passing.

"Where are we going?" she asked, knowing the answer.

"Home."

"Hank..."

"We'll talk when we get there," he interrupted softly. "It's long past time."

"Yes, it is," she replied. "There's something I must tell you." Hank gave her a strange look but said no more until they arrived at the house.

Laura felt a pang in her heart when he pulled to a stop. The house had always looked beautiful to her. With the landscaping finished, it looked perfect. The inside looked exactly the same as the last time she'd seen it; Hank hadn't altered as much as the position of one piece of furniture. Loving it, loving him, she moved slowly from room to room. A sad smile touched her mouth when she noticed the restored dining room and the new sliding glass panels. She had been cleaning up the mess when he'd...

"Laura, listen to me," Hank said urgently, gently taking her by the arms to turn her away from the former site of the debris and their debacle. "About that day," he began.

"You lied to me," she inserted. "You did want to hurt me, frighten me."

Hank looked straight into her eyes. "Yes, I lied. I was deliberately trying to hurt and frighten you."

"But why?" she cried. "What had I done?"

"Done?" A spasm of remorse flashed across his face. "Only the absolute worst thing a woman could do to me." He smiled when she shook her head in speechless confusion. "You made me want to feel again, Laura. You made me want to love again." He laughed shortly. "Oh, I was fighting it. It was tearing my guts out, but I was fighting it. Until that day. Something exploded in me when I heard my men and saw you there, looking so damned beautiful. The something that exploded in me, Laura, was jealousy and fear. A lethal combination.'' He paused as if the memory was clutching at his throat, making speech difficult. ''I was jealous of every man who looked at you, admired you, desired you. And I was so damned afraid I'd lose you, to some man, someday.''

You're mine, Laura. Mine. Remember it.

The echo of his words rang in her head and reverberated in her heart. ''Oh, Hank.'' Unashamed of the tears trickling down her cheeks. Laura raised her hand to stroke his face. ''Oh, my love. It wasn't necessary for you to hurt me or frighten me to keep me. I was yours from the beginning.''

A shudder ripped through his body. Closing his eyes, Hank pressed his lips against her palm. When he opened his eyes again, tiny drops of moisture clung to his blunt masculine lashes. ''I love you, Laura.'' His voice was thick, husky. ''I never thought I'd say that again to a woman. I never wanted to.'' His smile was shaky. ''Now, I want to beg you to let me say it to you for the rest of my life.''

Maybe she was a fool, Laura thought fleetingly. Maybe she was the world's biggest fool. She didn't care. Telling the world to back off, she launched herself into his arms. And then it seemed to her that one moment she was standing, crying, in the dining room, and the next moment she was flat on her back on the large bed in the master suite, holding her love tightly to her breasts.

''Say it.'' This time Hank wasn't insisting, he was pleading.

''I love you.''

''Oh, Laura, say it again and again and again.''

Laura said it over and over, breathlessly, moaning, the whole time they made love. The only time she stopped was when she cried out his name in ecstasy.

* * *

"Does your brother live here with you?"

"Yes." Hank drew a delicious shiver from her with his caressing lips and stroking hands.

"Will he continue to live here after we're married?"

His hands hesitated, his lips reluctantly moved away from her breasts. "Only for a few months. He's decided to relocate to the Pocono area." Hank lifted his head to look at her. "Do you object to having him stay with us?"

"No," Laura said, trailing her fingernails along his taut flank. "I was concerned that perhaps the baby's crying might annoy him," she explained, then held her breath.

"Crying?" Hank looked blank. Then he looked poleaxed. "Baby! Laura! You're pregnant?"

"If you'll remember," she said shakily, "I did say I had something to tell you."

"A baby." Hank still seemed slightly stunned. "We're going to have a baby?"

"Well, actually, I'm going to. Hank!"

He was hugging her, kissing her, laughing, crying. "A baby! Our baby! God, that's wonderful! You're wonderful! Oh, Laura, I love you."

She was crying, too. "I love you back."

* * * * *

Silhouette Desire ®

1989
IS THE YEAR
OF THE MAN!

What makes a romance? A special man, of course, and Silhouette Desire celebrates that fact with *twelve* of them! From Mr. January to Mr. December, every month has a tribute to the Silhouette Desire hero—our **MAN OF THE MONTH!**

Sexy, macho, charming, irritating . . . irresistible! Nothing can stop these men from sweeping you away. Created by some of your favorite authors, each man is custom-made for pleasure—*reading* pleasure—so don't miss a single one.

Mr. January is Blake Donavan in RELUCTANT FATHER by Diana Palmer
Mr. February is Hank Branson in THE GENTLEMAN INSISTS by Joan Hohl
Mr. March is Carson Tanner in NIGHT OF THE HUNTER by Jennifer Greene
Mr. April is Slater McCall in A DANGEROUS KIND OF MAN by Naomi Horton
Mr. May is Luke Harmon in VENGEANCE IS MINE by Lucy Gordon
Mr. June is Quinn McNamara in IRRESISTIBLE by Annette Broadrick

And that's only the half of it—
so get out there and find your man!

Silhouette Desire's

MAN OF THE MONTH . . .

ⅅ Silhouette Desire ®

COMING NEXT MONTH